Cold Fire

Shakespeare's Moon Act II

Cold Fire

Shakespeare's Moon Act II

James Hartley

LODESTONE
BOOKS

Winchester, UK
Washington, USA

First published by Lodestone Books, 2018
Lodestone Books is an imprint of John Hunt Publishing Ltd., No. 3 East Street,
Alresford, Hampshire SO24 9EE, UK
office1@jhpbooks.net
www.johnhuntpublishing.com

For distributor details and how to order please visit the 'Ordering' section on our website.

Text copyright: James Hartley 2017

ISBN: 978 1 78535 762 6
978 1 78535 763 3 (ebook)
Library of Congress Control Number: 2017944394

A CIP catalogue record for this book is available from the British Library.

Design: Stuart Davies

Printed and bound by CPI Group (UK) Ltd, Croydon, CR0 4YY, UK

We operate a distinctive and ethical publishing philosophy in
all areas of our business, from our global network of authors to
production and worldwide distribution.

For Han. For ever.

Also Available by James Hartley

The Invisible Hand *Shakespeare´s Moon ACT I*
(Lodestone Books, 978-1-78535-498-4)

Moods are the weather of the soul, Gillian thought.

The car was cresting a steep hill and beyond her elbow, through the open window, the Adriatic twinkled out to the melting sun. The road snaked ahead down the coast in a series of bumps and curves and the dry, olive-tree wind blowing through her hair cooled her sunburn.

I am a complete person, always the same, but I can be so different. I can be calm and perfect like the sea tonight or I can be dark and frightening like the sea at home. It all depends on my mood. And sometimes I can't control my moods. Sometimes everything is fine but I feel terrible. Sometimes the sun is shining but it rains inside. These days it always feels like it's raining. Everywhere.

Gillian concentrated on the music flooding from her white earbuds: anything except the real world. Anything except the argument she could see going on in the front seat. A hand was waving on one side, arms firmly crossed on the other, faces turning to bark in turn. They looked like animals when they were angry and snarling. Why couldn't they just shut their mouths and look at the beauty all around them? Or split up if everything was so bad? Why stay together and make each other unhappy?

I feel calm and content in myself. I am a planet moving through space, through the universe, as it should do, made up of many tiny parts. I am a gorgeous, chaotic creature connected to others both bigger and smaller. But the weather here on my planet is terrible. The storms are relentless. It's hard to enjoy this place in these conditions.

I'm like a beautiful city drowning under tides of melting ice.

I'm like a shimmering coral reef being suffocated by a floating island of plastic.

I'm a peaceful, sleepy town engulfed in the smoke of war.

I used to be happy.

I was happy when I was younger. I didn't even have to think about it, I just was. What planet was that?

I know I can be happy again. I have been happy once. I know what it is.

Otherwise what's the point of all this?
Why am I here?
Must I always hide inside? Deep inside, away from the sound of
the storms?

Later they sat at a white plastic table in the main square of a small town and had wagon-wheel pizzas. Gillian had never felt so miserable. Was there anything worse than feeling lonely when you were with your family? Feeling lonely when you were surrounded by the people you were supposed to love the most?

No one was talking. Mum was drinking red wine, her face changing only when the waiter approached: suddenly charming and quick to laugh. When he left, all the fake emotion dripped off her chin, her eyes rolled upwards and an ugly blankness swamped her features.

Dad sipped his beer, smoked his cigarettes and sometimes tipped up his phone to look at the screen. He seemed to hope Gillian wasn't noticing anything was wrong and occasionally asked: "Pizza alright, princess?" or "Want a top up?"

Gillian ate mechanically. As soon as possible she'd retreat back into the world of books or music, but first this. Slapping at nibbling mosquitoes. Wafting a sticky, laminated menu to ward off the stifling summer-night heat. Ignoring the local lads leering from mopeds as they droned by with loud, broken exhausts. "I'm going to the toilet," she said, walking towards the bar and straight into a noisy party.

Pushing through the boisterous crowd, some in fancy dress, Gillian came face to face with a gorilla mask. She stared into the eye-slits for what might have been eternity. Surprise, pleasure, knowledge, confusion, elation and then a gorgeous, warm current of connection passed between her and the eyes behind the mask. She knew him, somehow, the owner of those eyes. And he seemed to know her. She'd never felt as close to anyone as she did to that stranger.

Someone shouted: the barman.

The music came back: thumping, awful techno. The lights flashed purple, red and yellow and Gillian tasted dry ice. Someone jumped on the gorilla's back and almost knocked her out with a bottle of beer.

The bathrooms were dead ahead and her feet walked her there. When she came out the music was blaring and the bar was empty but for a mute television showing Italian football. Gillian squeezed by a skinny waiter coming in with a tray of drinks above his head. Outside was sweaty hot. Stars glowed in the night like phones at a concert.

Her father was counting out coins, holding them up to work out the denominations. "Your mum's gone back to the villa in a taxi," he reported, as if this was perfectly normal. "Do you want anything else before I pay up, princess? An ice cream or something?"

"No."

"Sure?"

"No. Can we just go?"

As she sat in the car, her father outside, leaning on the roof, making a call, Gillian looked out at the black, bejewelled sea. She couldn't imagine how it would be to float in the middle of it, lost among all that water, far away from the lights of the land, bobbing in the troughs of a slick, near-silent, liquid world. What loneliness that must be, to be lost in the middle of the sea!

Or to be the sea itself, sucked this way and that, free but bound, wild but trapped.

I want to be like the sea tonight, she told herself in her mind, in that same voice she'd spoken to herself with since she could remember. She felt in love and at peace with the calm, dark ocean; a part of it. *You are my real family,* she thought. *Nature is my real family.*

Gillian noticed the moon hanging low over the horizon and it seemed to cast a direct, bright-white trail, almost a pathway, across the waves to where she was.

For one weird moment she felt the urge to stand up, scramble down to the beach and run along that shining path right out to the moon. For a second it felt possible, as if the moon itself were urging her on. But then her father was climbing back inside the car smelling of smoke, the engine started and the spell was not only broken but well and truly smashed to bits.

Monday

1

Although it was July, the weather was awful. It had been since the start of term.

The rain dripping steadily from the brown, tattered clouds looked as though it had no intention of stopping. Rivulets trickled off sagging leaves and bored holes in the school rose-beds which spread soily puddles across the car park. The birds were in hiding. Delivery men used free newspapers as rain hats as they raced between their vans and the kitchens.

It was so dark they had the lights on in the dorm but Kizzie was smiling. *I'm in love*, she was thinking. *Finally!*

Kizzie pressed her nose to the window, her breath steaming the pane, and, looking directly downwards, watched Angela emerge from the Main Building. Her dorm-mate's dedication was incredible: training in this weather! Angela's lanky, white-socked, green-hooded figure set off into the drizzle, loped around the black semi-circle of driveway beneath the trees and vanished out through the main entrance.

"Who's nicked my new headphones?" shouted Priya from under her own bed. The dorm carpet, once red, was the colour of cardboard. Priya backed out, careful not to snag her hair on the springs, and held out her glinting, ringed fingers for an explanation.

"You've still got the price tag on your new shoes," Kizzie told her.

"I need my headphones, guys. It's not funny."

Kizzie, yawning operatically, started knotting her tie. "Not me."

"Athy borrowed them," came a sleepy Scottish voice from the top bunk by the door. "She left 'em in your sock drawer. Hid them in your Minnie Mouse specials if I'm not mistaken."

"Thanks Gillian." Priya fished out the tangle of white wires and opened the dorm door, wishing the girls a curt good morning. She came face to face with the Housemistress. "Oh. Hi, Miss Bainbridge."

"Kizzie?" Miss Bainbridge peered at them all from under a helmet of dry-looking, greyish hair. She always seemed to be wearing the same colours, if not the same clothes: frog, dog and an especially horrible shade of budgerigar. "Is she in here?"

"Yes, Miss B?"

"You're to report to the Headmaster's study straight after breakfast."

"Yes, Miss B." Kizzie nodded and noticed, out of the corner of her eye, Gillian's rumpled, bed-face peeping over her duvet. Priya was standing in the corridor behind Miss Bainbridge with a puzzled look on her pretty face, mouthing, *"What the...?"* as Kizzie asked, "Am I in trouble, miss?"

"No idea. That's for Mr Firmin to know and for you to find out, isn't it?"

"Yes, Miss B."

As Kizzie watched Miss Bainbridge slide away in her dirty, novelty slippers, Priya darted back inside the dorm and leaned against the dressing gowns hanging off the back of the door. "So? What was all that about?"

"What have you done, Kiz?" Gillian asked, upright on her bunk, her bare feet dangling from her too-short pyjama bottoms. Her short, dark hair was standing up in tufts. She'd been in such a deep sleep that all her features seemed to have crowded into the middle of her face. "Something bad. Has to be."

"Don't think so."

"You look guilty, to be honest, babe," noted Priya, bracelets jangling as she searched the tracks on her phone screen. "Your body language, I mean. Oh God, now that I say it, it's so obvious. You look *so* guilty."

"I *feel* guilty!" Kizzie replied, giggling. She always smiled when she was in trouble or nervous. When she was really nervous, on the verge of tears say, she had a habit of bursting into laughter. Like now.

"Well don't worry 'til you know, eh?" said Gillian. The bell for breakfast sounded in the corridor and Gillian groaned. "Oh, is that rain for real? What happened to summer?"

"Good Scottish weather that is, Gil," Priya told her, winking as she left. "You should feel right at home. I'll save you a place downstairs, girls. If it's the last time I ever see you, Kiz, it's been nice knowing you, all right? I'll send you the tenner I owe you to your new school, OK, babes?"

2

Angela took her usual route, jogging out through the main gate of the school and up the gravel lane directly opposite before turning right at the track which ran adjacent to the pony field.

Careful not to snag herself on the barbed wire, she skirted the field where the beehives where before stopping to walk through the graves in St Catherine's. At the far end of the churchyard, soaked to her knees with dew, she hopped the old, mossy stile and jogged up through the dripping bracken to where the footpath ringing the school known as The Gallops began.

Up above the first treeline, where tufts of cloud trailed off the leaves and branches below like smoke, Angela started her run proper. She set herself a decent pace and tried not to think about the rain or the niggling tightness in her left calf which had started during yesterday's run. The weather wasn't too much of a problem, she had the right gear on, but it made conditions underfoot slippery and unpredictable and she spent more time watching the ground than simply enjoying the run.

The path was slick with running water and sometimes the roots of the great oaks and elms that towered over were submerged or buried. The higher she went, the harder the rain pelted down and she ran with her arms stretched out, always ready to break her fall if she did go over. Somewhere in her mind she knew she should stop and walk but she couldn't bring herself to listen. *It'll be fine*, she thought, wiping a screen of rain off her face. *I'll be fine.*

This is wet rain, Angela thought, glancing up at the dull sky, remembering a phrase of her grandmother's. Wasn't all rain wet? But she understood what her grandmother had been getting at. It was horrible, thick, driving rain which worked its way up your nostrils and trickled down your collar and made you do that weird, jerky thing when it ran down your spine towards the small of your back.

At the top of the hill where the fences were, Angela went left rather than right, thinking she might cut the run short. A few minutes later she heard a train whistle from somewhere occluded but close by and realised she hadn't taken the path she thought she had. She'd run The Gallops many times so didn't panic but, checking her watch, she did worry about getting back in time for Assembly. She was only allowed out alone on condition she came back at the agreed times.

The mist and rain was too thick to be able to see far ahead – it was really *chucking it down* now – (her father's phrase, that one) – so when she spotted a narrow path darting off downhill she took it, ducking under a broken, dripping bough and slithering side-footed through soaking green ferns and nettles. Cold droplets sprayed up into her eyes and she felt twigs and loose stones whip her ankles.

Any way down is good, Angela thought, mildly out of control. *I'll get to the bottom, find the bypass and jog back to the school. Stupid to come out in this weather. What was I thinking?*

Angela spotted something in her juddering, peripheral vision further down the steep path, blocking her way. She couldn't look up long enough to see what it was. A sixth sense warned her of danger.

It's a person. A man.

This didn't immediately register: it seemed impossible that she could come face to face with someone up here, in the rain, in the middle of nowhere.

But it *was* someone: a balding man in a sopping, white, baggy shirt with a leather waistcoat and straggly, long hair. The stranger opened his blue diamond eyes with surprise as Angela came hurtling towards him. As they collided Angela put both hands to her head, closed her eyes and screamed.

She felt a coldness, like the wind when a train passes close by.

Eyes still closed, blind, screaming, Angela ran on as fast as she could. She was shivering all over, from the inside out. Panting, frantic, she blinked her eyelids open and narrowly avoided a spiked tree trunk, bounding around it, out of control, unable to stop even if she'd wanted to, careering ever onwards down a hill which seemed to steepen in gradient with every wild, bouncing step.

Oh no.

And after a moment's silence – a moment of flight – she crash landed, hitting the ground with a nasty crunch, falling hard. She felt and heard scratching and thrashing as the uneven ground stopped her dead.

Ow.

Fear and adrenalin got Angela upright: she examined her own hands as though she were a robot, opening and closing her fingers in front of her wide eyes. She knew from somewhere that the fact she could move them meant they weren't broken.

The man!

She looked uphill, bleeding, panting.

Nothing. Long green shoots. So very green, lurid almost, with that grim, black, thundery sky behind them. More trees further uphill, alive, shaking their leaves, but no human movement. What had tripped her?

Blood on her knee. Grazed elbows. Some kind of dull pain on her cheekbone. Heart thumping. And then a noise over the pants: *oh, sweet sound of safety!*

Angela had heard the steady hum of the morning rush-hour traffic shooting along the bypass.

3

Kizzie was examining the pictures on the walls outside the Headmaster's office, being nosy.

Various old Heads of St Francis's scattered the walls and she righted the frames that were slightly askew. There was an aerial view which Kizzie knew had been taken in summer because she could make out the blue rectangle of the school pool. Her eyes drifted across the panelled wall to a small painting which might have been a bible scene or – *ah, yes, of course*, Kizzie thought – *Cleopatra and some Roman. Julius Caesar? Mark Antony?* She got a shock as she noticed a strange old lady lurking in the shadows at the back of the picture who was the spitting image of her sister Athy.

"Kizzie!"

Turning, Kizzie saw her boyfriend Zak coming down the corridor towards her, a big grin on his face. "What are you doing up here?" she hissed. "Dressed like that, too! Firmin will have a heart attack if he sees you."

Zak was in a grey trench coat, the shoulders black with rain. He wore a beige fedora hat, also stained, and cowboy boots, but, as he told her, was otherwise in regulation school uniform and couldn't see what the problem was. "Priya just gave me a heads up on what's happening. I wanted to come and wish you luck, that's all." Zak grinned and Kizzie felt the corners of her own mouth lifting in response.

"Nutter."

"Are you OK?" Zak put a hand on her arm.

"I am, I am. Thank you. But go! You're going to get both of us in trouble. Go, go!"

"What's funny?"

Kizzie tried to control her wild smile, which only made it worse. "Nothing! Just go, will you! You're making me worse!"

"*Ohhh* kay." Zak backed away. "I'll wait for you downstairs at the Steps." He assumed a very serious expression. "By the way, I hope you put two pairs of undies on in case, you know –" he faked a caning – "Whack! Whack!"

"Go!"

"Did you?"

"No!"

"Ooh, beginner's mistake, Kiz. It's gonna hurt. Want a stick or something to bite down on? A pencil?" Now at the end of the corridor Zak, pretending to search his pockets, blew Kizzie a kiss, made a strong-arm gesture and disappeared. Kizzie heard his cowboy boots clip-clopping their way down the staircase and turned back to the oak door.

She raised her hand to knock but suddenly became aware of a weird thudding sound coming from behind her, like monster's footsteps. Turning, she was about to scream at Zak when she caught sight of the wretched figure of Angela, face bloodied, holding her own elbow with her only good hand, hobbling across the landing on two skinny white legs grazed at the knees. "Oh my God! What happened to you?" Kizzie cried.

Angela waved Kizzie's help away and said she was going to surgery. "Nothing's going on. I'm just clumsy, me. As usual. Just clumsy."

"You should see Matron. Now."

Angela nodded. "I'm going." She raised an eyebrow. "What are you doing here?"

"Have to see Firmin."

"What have you done?"

Kizzie shrugged. "Dunno."

Angela thought about this but suddenly winced at a fresh pain. "Well, good luck." She shuffled on towards the door of the girl's house and let out a loud breath as she turned the handle. Whatever superpower had got her up off the ground, over the road and through the school grounds was now wearing off and everything was starting to throb and hurt. Despite this, before going to the surgery – she could see the door was open and hear Radio Two booming out as usual – she went into the dorm and walked right up to the window.

Whoever he was, Angela hoped the man she'd seen up in the hills was all right. He'd seemed weirdly familiar. The whole thing had been so weird. What was he doing up there dressed like that? Probably a nutter. Some people said the big house at the top of The Gallops, the one that was fenced off, was an Asylum, or hospital, or whatever you called them now.

Angela liked her dark reflection in the window. It was so much gentler than the mirror proper. No glowing zits. No weird, pointed ears. No odd, square, mannish jaw and jutting teeth.

In the dark reflection she looked like she wanted to look, not harsh and grotesque like she was in reality.

4

"Ah, there you are, Jull-Costa. Come in, come in."

Kizzie was grinning like The Joker. She held her hands pressed onto the front of her skirt to stop them trembling. "Hello, Headmaster. Everyone." Her eyes flickered around the faces. She knew Mr Firmin quite well. He'd taught her last year. He was standing at the bay window at the far end of the room in his usual white linen suit, smiling but serious, listing slightly, as he always did, as though he was on the deck of a ship. Kizzie also recognised Sam and Leana, the Head Boy and Girl, and Alain Verne, the leader of The Magistrate. The three prefects were smiling up at her from their seats in front of the fire.

"Come and sit here," Leana said to Kizzie, patting an empty space on the dark leather sofa. The Head Girl's eyes were friendly, though guarded, and it put Kizzie at ease. She did as she was told and they all looked up at Firmin, who had come around to the front of his desk and was examining the tip of his well-chewed pipe.

"Apologies if we've made you feel uneasy, Kizzie," the Headmaster began. "This meeting is a little something I like to do with all those who are about to be promoted to The Magistrate. A chance to clear the air, have a little informal chat, as it were, before announcements become *official* and the whole rigmarole is put in place."

"Sorry, sir?" Kizzie asked, startled. "Did you say something about promotion?"

"Yes," nodded Mr Firmin, grinning. He had a clipped, neat moustache and, when he was happy, like now, his whole face was lit up by a warm, paternal smile. "That's right, my dear."

"Congratulations, Kizzie," Sam told her, holding out his hand.

Leana, closer, hugged Kizzie and whispered, "Welcome!"

"Now the way we do this is as follows. Alain will be your shadow today." Mr Firmin pointed to the Head of the Magistrate with his pipe. "He'll have a little chat with you this morning and try to answer your questions and help you reach a decision. You have about twenty-four hours –" Firmin checked a timepiece he'd dug out of his waist-coat – "to give us your answer. If we hear nothing from you to the contrary, we'll expect you in the Eleusinian Room this time tomorrow morning for the investiture. How does that sound?"

"Oh." Kizzie didn't know what to say.

"Just take your time," Leana whispered to her. "Have a chat with Alain. Think about it."

"I thought we might take a little walk now?" Alain said, leaning across and showing her his empty palms. "You are excused Assembly. The school will be quiet. Only the rain to worry about."

"Fine. Yes. That sounds fine." Kizzie felt as though she were in a dream. Sam, Leana and Alain were people she'd only ever seen from afar, on the stage at school in Assembly, passing by in an untouchable bubble or eating at The Magistrate's table in the dining hall. It was odd to see them here, so close and being so freakily friendly. "Are you sure this is right?" she asked them all. "You've got the right person?"

"Of course it is!" Leana laughed. "And you're going to be one of the youngest ever members of The Magistrate, if you accept. You should be very proud."

"Well," drawled the Headmaster, wringing his big hands. "Perhaps I should be getting across to the Assembly Hall. Try to keep word of all this to yourself for now, Jull-Costa, if you wouldn't mind. At least until you've made a decision."

"Yes, sir," said Kizzie, nodding. "Of course."

"Good morning to you all then."

5

Alain Verne turned his collar up as he stood with Kizzie on the back step of the Main Building. "Can we risk not taking an umbrella?" he wondered aloud. "It's stopping now. Do you think it will hold?"

Kizzie felt very self-conscious and gabbled, "Let's just go. Bit of rain never hurt anyone. Not like we're going to shrink, is it?"

She walked a step behind the prefect, aware that just across the pathway, outside the Assembly Hall, queuing to go in, she'd been spotted. Gillian, Priya, Angela and Athy were nudging each other and turning to gawp. Kizzie tried to show with a smile that she wasn't in trouble – *it's all right! He's not frog marching me out of school!* – but at the same time Alain made a gesture with his leather-gloved hand, the merest waggle, which sent the girls and all the other onlookers into the Assembly Hall without a backward glance.

It was strange, Kizzie thought, to walk around the school with someone who had such an effect on other people. She was used to being half-invisible, standing in lines, crushed up against others, waiting all the time, sitting or standing near the back of the class, in the huddle and muddle of things. But now people moved out of their way. People did double takes and smokers sneaking back from the fields darted head-first into bushes at the merest sight of them.

She felt slightly ashamed and self-conscious but *boy* it was fun.

"So," Alain said, holding out his arms as they walked down towards the place called The Dips, a series of mud hills near the red-brick perimeter wall of the school. "As you probably know, this is the oldest part of the school, where the first buildings on the site were built." Kizzie immediately knew she was listening to a speech he'd made more than once before. "Next year we were thinking of marking the school's anniversary down here. Perhaps putting up a marquee or a stage. Reclaiming it from the smokers and lovers. Trouble is –" the head prefect gestured towards the heavens – "One never knows what the weather will be like, as you can see."

Kizzie noticed two sycamore trees which rose from the dirty-copper mud and whose branches interlocked, creating an ad-hoc shelter used for the various illegal purposes Alain had alluded to. "How come they didn't just build the school here?" she asked, recognising with a jolt some initials carved into one of the trunks. She turned her back to cover them and save Priya's life.

"The road is too close," Alain told her. "It's always been a main road. A public path, thoroughfare, turnpike. Now a bypass." As they listened, they could both hear the steady drone of cars passing by. It was always there if you listened out for it but thankfully most of the time you could ignore it. Nature seemed louder, somehow. "It was easier to move everything uphill, especially in recent times. This all used to be farmland." Alain pointed uphill, towards the tennis courts. "The best land was up there, where the Assembly Hall is. Oh, I think this rain is getting worse. Come on. Let's get under the trees over there."

As they walked quickly towards the playing fields, along the back of the dripping tennis-court chicken fencing, Alain asked Kizzie if she knew why she had been offered the chance of joining The Magistrate.

"Because I've been helping a lot in the library?" Kizzie answered, laughing. She'd been nervously awaiting the question ever since she'd heard the news in Firmin's study. Now her face alternated between manic happiness and a kind of grief. Her real feelings were somewhere in the middle. "Maybe that?"

"No, no." Alain tutted and ticked his finger from side to side like a pendulum. "No, no, no."

Kizzie giggled horribly. It was more like a cough than a laugh. They were coming to the wet wooden fence at the edge of the fields where green-and-white-shirted boys would be soon go trudging out through the dew to play football. In the distance lay the Pavilion, half rubbed out by the drizzle, and Kizzie shivered when she realised she'd be walking out there to play hockey in an hour or so.

"It's because of last term's English class results, Kizzie. The girls' results specifically."

Kizzie was relieved and confused. "I don't get it."

"All the girls passed."

"Ah, did they? Did we?"

"Yes, yes. And all with stories about the same family. Interlinking stories. Surely you haven't forgotten? Miss Christie was very impressed. So impressed, in fact, that she asked me to have a look at the work."

"We didn't cheat, if that's what you're getting at!"

"I know you didn't cheat." Alain laughed.

"We just talked about it before. Together. Brainstorming."

"Ah, but from what I understand, *you* imagined all of the characters; all of the stories?"

"More or less." Kizzie honestly couldn't remember. The whole class had stayed behind one lunchtime and talked about ideas. Perhaps she had taken the main role but it had been more of a sharing of ideas. "But I didn't write their essays for them. I swear."

"The ability to believe in and share ideas is unique to human beings, Kizzie," Alain said gravely, turning to face her as he leaned back against the fence. "You have the ability to inspire people, to make them believe and see worlds that you have created. It's a very important, powerful talent."

"Thank you."

"Much depends on the personality who wields a talent like yours. Some people use it for selfish reasons, simply to show off or perform, some for manipulating others, the worst of all possible uses. You understand the best way to use the skill you have. Yes, although you might not have thought about it in such a way, you have shown us your personality, Kizzie: the type of person you are. *That* is why we've asked you to join The Magistrate."

"Thank you," Kizzie repeated. Again, she didn't know what else to say. "Great."

Alain, who was looking at her with a rather cheesy smile, suddenly clapped his gloves together. "All right. That's the serious part." He laughed, bounced up off the fence and held out his arm, indicating that they should walk together up to the main path.

"Can I have a bit of time just to think about things?" Kizzie asked, glad to be out of the mud and onto concrete.

"Of course, of course!"

"Just to, you know, think a bit. Get my thoughts straight."

"Yes, yes. Of course, of course."

They walked on in an awkward silence. Kizzie began to speak but Alain started at the same time and she was happy to smile and say, "After you. Please."

"No, it's only that I do, actually, have one more question." The prefect was suddenly shy, smaller somehow and Kizzie was surprised to realise he was nervous. "It's a personal question. I will be speaking in a personal capacity, if I may?"

Kizzie buried her chin in her scarf and raised her eyebrows. "Oh-kay."

"It's not about you," Alain said, a little too quickly. He walked around in front of Kizzie, noticing her attention had wandered, walking backwards. "I don't mean that badly. I don't mean it's not about *you*. I mean, it's about someone you know. A question, really. Nothing more. Personal, as I say. About a friend of yours."

Kizzie looked at the blonde-fringed prefect standing before her with his badge, his perfectly tied scarf, handsome chin, gelled hair and plucked eyebrows and felt powerful. "Go on, then."

"This friend of yours," Alain began, falling back in to line alongside Kizzie. The hulk of the red-brick Assembly Hall now appeared ahead of them, to the right of the path. The school was quiet: everyone was in the Hall and there was a thin, cold mist in the air.

"Yes?"

"And you must understand, again, that I am asking you this in a personal capacity, not as the leader of The Magistrate." Alain seemed to lose his nerve and spoke to himself quickly in French, something Kizzie didn't understand. A second later he was in front of her with a very serious look on his face, wiping his high forehead free of three stiff hairs. "I need to know about Gillian Shelley. Your friend. Gillian."

"Ah-ha," said Kizzie, nodding. "I see. Righto. Well, go on, then. What do you want to know?"

"I want to know if she would be interested in me," said the prefect, very directly. It was bravado but it had obviously worked before. A kind of bald arrogance. He smiled, bowing slightly.

"Interested? What do you mean?"

"In a relationship." Alain couldn't look her in the eye. "To be...with me? To – to make a couple?"

"Ah, OK. Like *that*."

"Like that."

"OK, I'll ask her," replied Kizzie, eyes wide, slightly shocked.

"*Bon*." Alain nodded.

They were at The Steps now, a convergence of pathways, the main intersection and meeting place of the school. Alain morphed back into the prefect he'd been for the first part of their walk. He sniffed, whacked the fingers of his gloves into each other and flicked the hair off his fringe with confidence. Kizzie remained still. She wasn't quite sure what had just happened.

"Very well, Miss Jull-Costa," Alain said, holding out a rigid hand. "It was a great pleasure to meet you and it will be a great pleasure to lead you in The Magistrate, should you chose to accept."

Kizzie shook his hand. "Lovely." She nodded. "I'll get back to you very soon."

"I would appreciate it." Backing up, Alain laughed, crouched and cocked his gloved fingers into pistols. "On both matters, eh?"

Kizzie nodded, wanting to be alone. "Gotcha," she replied, making a similar shooting gesture for some reason she'd never know. She turned around and walked away with her face scrunched up in embarrassment.

6

Lunchtime in the dining hall was noisy and crowded. Someone had drawn a huge heart in the condensation on one of the long windows and there were queues at the tea urn, the toaster and at the small hatch where trays and leftovers were deposited. A steady stream of tray-wielding students came out from the food-counter exit and stood near the teacher's table as they searched out their friends. Although the rain had stopped, the white floor was scuffed with muddy shoeprints and cardboard had been put down over the wettest areas.

"Oh, here comes Her Majesty," remarked Sol Kerouac as Kizzie approached. "All rise, please! All rise! You do us plebs a great honour, my Queen."

Kizzie rolled her eyes. "Oh, very funny, Sol." She looked accusingly at Priya, Angela, Athy and Gillian. "You lot promised you wouldn't say anything! I'm not supposed to tell anyone, remember. Honestly. Can't say anything to anyone here without it becoming common knowledge."

"We won't say anything," Zak assured Kizzie, pulling out a chair for her. Zak and Sol were mates but polar opposites: Sol was dark, muscular and sarcastic; Zak, blonde, pale and humble. "We know how to keep secrets. We're friends, right? Besides, none of us know Priya has Minnie Mouse knickers, do we?" His sniggering was stopped by a clout on the head.

"Shut it!"

"Leave Kizzie alone, guys," Angela said as Priya continued to attack Zak. "You're only jealous."

"Jealous? Yeah, that's right," mocked Sol. "That's it. You've hit the nail on the head there, Mummy." He pointed at Angela's copy of *Romeo and Juliet,* open beside her tray. "How can you read that crap for pleasure, anyway? You see!" He gestured to the others. "That's another example of what I've been saying. A perfect example! Brainwashed by this stupid idea that just keeps on selling!"

Angela, bandaged up – hence the Mummy jibe – shook her head. "It's homework, you idiot."

"But you *laaav* it."

"Kiz," Angela said, turning away from Sol's drooping, flapping tongue. "You're not going to believe what he's been going on about this morning."

"What now?"

Two silver hearts sparkled beneath the curtains of Angela's brown hair. "Go on, then, Sol. Carry on with what you were saying."

Sol shrugged. "What? I haven't said anything that's not true, have I?" Beside him on the table was Zak's beige fedora hat and gloves. "I'm not saying love doesn't exist *at all*. I'm just saying that it's not something, I dunno, airy-fairy. It's there for a purpose, you know. It's not as weird as it's made out to be. It's definitely not something that comes from the sky, or God, or happens to you if you're lucky or unlucky."

Kizzie examined Zak while pretending to be exasperated with Sol: there was a hint of golden stubble on his chin and his eyes were lovely. "What do you think, Zak?"

"Oh, I'm a sucker for love," Zak replied, too shy to look up and show if he meant it or not.

"If it's ever proved that love doesnae exist," Gillian joined in, "then about a million rubbish musicians are going to be out of a job, I'll tell you that."

"*Doesnae*," Sol echoed, chuckling, whacking his fingers together so they made a cracking noise. "Love it. Classic Scotch brogue there, Gil."

Gillian turned away towards the window with her tea. "You're a child."

"Och, come on, lassie. You ken I love you, don't ye?"

"Sooo tedious," Gillian drawled, examining the heart

dribbling down the window beside her.

"There'd be no more rom-coms either, if you think about it," Kizzie noted, breaking the crusts off her toast.

"Watch it! I love rom-coms," Angela warned them, wincing as she raised a hand. "You leave 'em alone. There's way more horrible things in the world than rom-coms."

"The thing I don't get about those movies," Sol said, "is that they always finish with the wedding, the bit where they get together. Someone always realises that they've made a mistake, usually the man, and then there's a long running scene – better if it's at Christmas or in cold weather – he makes it, she takes him back, they kiss and that's the end. It's always the same."

"And football isn't?" Gillian sniggered.

Sol held up a finger. "Don't go there, lassie. Don't go there. I'll haggis yer stovies off!"

"It's all about the chase, though, isn't it?" Kizzie turned at a commotion behind them. One of the pink-faced kitchen staff was leaning out of the serving hatch shouting angrily at a boy who'd run off, blue coat dragging along the wet floor.

"But do they all have to be exactly the same?" Sol waved a slice of dry-looking pie through the air. "*Exactly* the freakin' same?"

Gillian rubbed her eyes. "It sells, Sol. People like it." She tapped the end of her nose to stop herself sneezing. "And why do you say 'movies' anyway? That's an American word. You're English, aren't you?"

"It's an American art form," answered Sol.

"No, it isn't," Gillian began. "The first films were French."

Sol swore and pulled out his phone to Google it. Gillian examined his face. Sol had his tongue out, concentrating. Unaware that he was being watched, not posing, as he usually did, Gillian thought he looked incredibly brutish and dumb.

I can't believe he's brought his phone in here, Athy, Kizzie's younger sister, was thinking, impressed. Sol really was the most brazen, shameless, shocking boy in the school. *And he's using it!*

"But do you really believe what you were saying before, though, Sol?" Angela asked, butting in. "About love only being biological? Or were you just trolling?"

"Of course I believe it," Sol replied, thumbs busy under the table-top. "We – humans, I mean – need to trust each other, to work together and survive. We're just monkeys after all. That's all it is. Love's just a feeling, man, like, a chemical reaction, to make sure we don't kill each other. It keeps us together, makes sure we look after our babies. It's a survival thing, nothing more."

Angela wrinkled her nose. "That's so cold and horrible."

"Why?" Sol cried. "Better to know the truth, surely? Too many people waste their lives waiting for some weird thing they've seen in movies – sorry, Gil, *films* – and heard about in songs. If only they realised how simple it all really was, they could have it too."

"People always seem to think it starts with, like, this great burst of passion." This was Athy, who reddened as they all turned to look at her, but managed to continue, staring down at the orange she was peeling, which spat juice and smelled of summer. "I think love can take ages to get going sometimes. I don't think it always has to be this great physical thing. I think it can build up over time. As you get to know someone, I mean. It can kind of grow."

"If you think about it," Sol went on, piling the empty plates and crumpled napkins on his tray as the others murmured their agreement with Athena, "it's all biology, that's all. We're monkeys, man. Animals. *Beasts!* We do what we have to do; what we've had to do, to survive."

"Oh, wow!" Athena cried as Zak stood up with Sol. "You're wearing cowboy boots, Zak!"

"I surely am, ma'am," Zak replied, raising his hat and standing.

"Pony care for you this term, then, is it?" Angela muttered, sipping tea. The others chuckled.

"Leave him alone," Kizzie said. "Ignore them, Zak."

Sol made a joke about 'rides' and the boys left with Sol draped over Zak's shoulder like he'd been shot. As well as cowboy boots, Zak caused heads to turn with his hat. He was the only boy in the school to wear one. As they crashed out into the wet, cold morning, Sol pulled out the cigarette he had behind his ear and two girls passing by stopped to let he and Zak go past as if they were stars.

"Are you all right, Gil?" Kizzie put a hand on her friend's shoulder. Gillian was very serious, her face pinched beneath her short hair. She held a cup under her chin but was staring straight ahead through the steam. "Holidays all right?"

"No. Horrible."

"Oh God. Why?"

Gillian's eyes momentarily glazed over but she controlled herself. "Ah, nothing. The usual. Home. Parents. All the fun of the fair, you know."

"Your mum?"

"Both of them, really. My mum's the worst. I feel like I'm about ten every time I'm with her, like a kid. Nothing I do is right. Neither of them ever say anything to encourage me, only criticise." Gillian's eyes moistened. "Honestly, it's pathological sometimes, like they hate me, you know." She wanted to stop but the words wanted out. "Mum attacks but dad doesn't defend. He's scared of her, like everyone. Like me, probably. But that's how she likes it."

"Sounds horrible," Kizzie replied gently.

"Honestly, when I come back here I feel like me again, if that makes sense. There I can't be me. I'm some version of me who can't say what they really feel."

"Maybe your mum's just unhappy," tried Athy.

"Both of them, I'd say," added Angela, nodding.

"Aye, maybe," nodded Gillian. "But I've tried, you know. But she – mum – moves the goalposts. If I sort one problem out, she finds another. Sometimes she changes whole stories, you know. I come home and she's thought up all these new things I've done wrong. Everyone's out for her, you know. She's got something on everyone."

"At least you've got your mum," Angela said. It wasn't said to make Gillian feel guilty but because she – Angela – felt she had to say it. "We used to fight but I'd give anything to have her back for a day now."

"Aye, right. I'm sorry, Ange. I didn't mean it like it sounds." But Gillian *had* meant it like that. For some reason things were getting worse at home, almost unbearable. It had gotten so bad that she'd wished her mother dead more than once. Quickly, not painfully. Just gone. Out of her life. She wanted to be free.

"You know she can only have an effect on you if you let her," Kizzie said.

"What do you mean?"

"That your life is your life, you know. I mean, we get things from our parents, sure, but it doesn't have to trap us. We can choose what we're like. Change the things we don't like."

Gillian was about to argue but then she said, "I think that would be the worst thing ever. Seriously. Turning into her. Blaming the whole world for everything."

"Then don't," Kizzie said.

Gillian's eyes went glassy. "Hard," she said, her lips thinning. "Another thing I don't get: they're always tired. From their jobs. Tired. Too much work. Tired, tired. I don't get why they do it. Oh, wait, I do get it. They do it for me. So I can get a good education and get a job like them and be tired all the time, I guess." Gillian threw up her hands. "I don't get it at all. I don't get it; it's like madness. Everyone's mad, just following what everyone else is doing!"

"Happy happy," said Kizzie.

"What the hell have you got in your hair?" Gillian asked, touching Kizzie's afro-like, blonde fuzz, blatantly changing the subject. Kizzie's hair, as usual, was embroidered with wraps and dangling pendants.

"Magic stuff!"

"Can you imagine if love *really* didn't exist, though?" wondered Athy out loud, taking up the thread of the old conversation again. Athena was a smaller, prettier version of her big sister Kizzie; where Kizzie's look was Einstein-mad, Athena's was more chic and controlled. Athena was shy and withdrawn, sure of herself at heart; Kizzie was the exact opposite.

Gillian checked her phone. "Oh, you lot are obsessed." Half an hour to the last double period of the day: Maths. *Yippee!* "You're as pathetic as the films. You really think a guy – or love, for that matter – will make you happy? You're looking in the wrong place!" The bitter tone of this little outburst changed the mood between the friends.

"It's only a bit of fun," Angela said. "What d'you prefer? That we sit staring into our tea and saying how crap the world is?"

Gillian shook her head. "No. Sorry." She couldn't put into words what she was thinking. The summer had been awful. Being with her parents had kicked up a storm in her soul that hadn't settled. She didn't know how she felt. All she wanted to do was disappear. Be quiet. Be on her own. "Sorry, forget it. I'm just…"

The girls turned at a commotion from the window beside them. Two Year Nine girls, wrapped in scarves were outside waving their hands.

"What are they saying?" Kizzie asked.

Gillian, who was nearest the window, shrugged her shoulders, wiped off part of the heart and mouthed: *We can't hear you!*

One of the Year Nine girls, after consulting with the other, began to write on the smudged, steamed-up glass.

Gradually the message took shape:

THEЯE'S A NAꓘED BOY ON TH∃ PLAYIN⅁ ꓇IELꓤS

7

By the time the girls reached the fields they could see a small crowd of students near the centre circle of the football pitch. The day had not really risen, more fallen out of bed. It was muggy and close, half-asleep and oddly quiet. The sun was up behind the far-off clouds, shining like a torch under a bed sheet.

"Maybe we should just leave the poor guy alone?" Gillian said, at the lip of the wet turf. Something about the situation scared her, aroused some weird animal instinct in her. Fear, perhaps. Trepidation. She felt as though she were walking towards an accident; that she was going to see something horrible, something she might never be able to unsee.

"What?" Athy laughed. "Are you joking? I'm going. This is the coolest thing to happen here in ages."

"Me too," Angela added, setting off with Athena after Zak and Sol. Zak's long brown coat flapped out behind him as he strode forward with his hands in pockets. Athy looked back, excitement in her eyes, and gestured for the other two to get moving.

Kizzie, like Gillian, wasn't so keen. "Who do you think it is?"

"I dunno," Gillian said, "but whoever it is, they can't want us all gawping and staring at them."

"Do you think anyone's told the teachers?"

"Aye." Gillian looked back once and tucked her chin into her scarf. "For sure."

"Actually, Gil. Can you come here a sec?" More pupils were now walking down towards them, chattering, and Kizzie stepped off the path and led them both to the wooden fence. "I've got something to ask you."

Gillian cocked an eyebrow. "Now?"

"Probably the only chance we'll be alone for a while."

"What is it?"

"You know Alain Verne?"

"The guy you were talking to this morning? The Magistrate guy?"

"Yep."

"Aye."

"Well, he likes you."

"What?" Gillian took a step back, grinned and pulled a face. She pointed the tip of her black shoe in the mud and drew a circle. Verne was roundly considered to be the best-looking boy in the school – the top dog – but as a sixth former he was out of bounds to Gillian and her friends. He might as well have been a famous actor or musician.

"Gil, I'm serious. He was asking me about you this morning. He proper likes you. He wants to go out with you and everything."

This time Gillian did force a snigger. "Oh, Kiz, come on. How did all this come up? I thought you were talking about the Magistrate and stuff?"

"We were, we were, but then he asked about you."

"Mental." Gillian sighed, shaking her head. She looked up at the huddle in the centre of the football pitch and it morphed into a group of mourners gathered around an open grave. She felt a repulsion, as though she should wake away. Turn around and keep going. Never look back.

Later she would realise what it all meant, it would all make sense, but now it was only a cold, warning feeling. Like hearing a voice, somewhere inside, telling you to not do something. Same as that odd feeling when you knew someone was thinking about you, or when you knew someone was hiding in what looked like an empty room, or when someone was about to make contact.

"So?"

"So, what?"

"Gil! So, what do you think?"

"What do I think about what? About going out with Verne?"

"Yes!" Kizzie noticed Angela coming back towards them,

jogging over the wet, muddy grass. She had the lithe, taut gait of a long-distance runner, despite her injuries.

"No!" Gillian replied. "Are you serious, Kiz? No, no, no. A million times, no."

"Because he's too old?"

"No!"

"Then what?"

"Because..." Gillian ducked to yank up her tights at the knee. She talked to herself, turning in circles. "I don't like him, that's what. Not that way. No one could ever like him more than he likes himself anyway, so it's a no-go." Her face crumpled as she rose. "No!"

Kizzie giggled. "You could carry his mirror and comb for him."

"Exactly." Gillian shivered. "Oh God, could you imagine?"

Angela arrived, breathless. "He's not from school, the bloke. He's naked. Speaking in some foreign language. Seriously. I'm not joking. Totally naked. Like, *nothing* on. Latin or something. Really weird."

"Latin?" Kizzie looked at Gillian.

Gillian, who'd spent the last term studying Latin on a whim, had an odd, blank look on her face. "Oh, no, no. I don't know anything. Fabritzia would be better." Fabritzia was the only other girl in the Latin class. She was Italian and had chatted with the teacher as Gillian had read the graffiti on the desks.

"Fabritzia's sick, remember," Angela replied impatiently. "Mono. She didn't come back this term. Anyway, come on, come on!"

The girls set off somewhere between running and walking. The bare winter trees poked up from the perimeter of the fields like hands from graves.

As the girls came closer they saw the naked boy sitting hunched over, facing away from them. His cold-looking, greyish skin was taut on his shoulders and back. He looked about their age and had his knees drawn up, his bare toes flecked with grass. Gillian realised she was holding her breath. Every sense in her body, every nerve and neuron was agitated, and she knew she had to see the face of the youth even if it meant something horrible: for there was to be a horrible revelation, she forefelt it.

"Totally amazing," laughed Zak, coming over to them. "He just keeps saying, like, two sentences. It's like he fell out of the sky or something."

"Gyppo," Sol smirked, spitting.

Gillian left the others behind and felt completely alone, in perfect silence, with the boy. She joined the queue of pupils, passing alongside and before the youth – that funereal thing again! – and as she came around in front of him she reached the apex of trepidation. His dark hair was cut short and the strands of his wet fringe spiked down to his cheekbones. As he looked up, as if knowing she was there, they met eye to eye and all fear evaporated.

Love poured into Gillian's soul and his eyes smiled at her again – again, because it was him: the boy she remembered from Italy, from the holiday, from the bar – and she smiled right back. She couldn't help it! Somewhere behind her shoulders Gillian could hear people speaking, like voices underwater, but she couldn't remove her gaze from his.

Looking into the boy's eyes she saw the universe she'd come from, that she belonged in. His black pupils were great planets with fiery, divine halos encircling them. Shards of silver, slate and Ionian blue drew her close to his face and their lips sealed the bargain their eyes and souls had struck.

"...back, Gil – there's people coming!"

Gillian heard voices, caught her breath, and rocked back on her haunches. The words of the others were as loud and frightened. Standing, she looked down at the shivering, grey shape of the boy and tore off her coat, shirking clear of Kizzie long enough to drape it around his shoulders before the other girl got her away, pulling her free of the crowd.

A group of prefects were now circling the sitting boy, facing outwards, arms joined at the elbows like policemen ordering the pupils back and away, back and away, back and away, and Kizzie led Gillian – who was dazed and wide-eyed and pale – back to their group. "I got her just in time," she reported to the others.

"Gillian, what the hell?" asked Angela, her hand over her mouth.

"That was top class, really, Gil." Zak laughed. "Amazing stuff."

"Tongues and everything," added Sol, clicking his fingers. "Straight in there, man!"

They began to drift back with the other pupils, back towards the path, the Assembly Hall, double Maths and normality, and soon Gillian was shaking her head and saying that she didn't know what had happened to her, but of course she did.

She could feel the afterburn of his lips on hers. She could feel the meshing of their souls, like smoke with smoke, and knew he was with her; that they were connected now. In her heart and soul she was happy and it was an odd feeling; something she was not used to.

I am different, she thought. And she was.

I am not the same girl who walked down here ten minutes ago. And she wasn't.

8

Miss Tartt's nickname was The Bell because of an old haircut she'd long since ceased to live under. The name had been given to her years back, not long after she'd arrived at St Francis's, and had been passed down through the years. She knew it well and considered it not half as bad as it might have been. The only thing that niggled her was the way she would hear pupils whispering "ding dong" at her as she approached. Some of the bolder boys might shout it from doorways or windows where they were hiding.

She looked out at her class from behind her dark lashes and matt-black shiny hair. As usual she was wearing a sombre-coloured business suit, this time with thin white lapels and a brooch. In her long-fingered, purple-nailed hands she was holding a copy of *Romeo and Juliet* and was repeating, "Page three. Page three everyone. Page three, if you would all be so kind. If anyone would be so kind. If anyone would even listen to me. Is anyone listening to me? Does anyone know what Page Three even is? I'm doing this for you, people. I've read this book. I know this stuff. I know what's on Page Three – do you?"

Angela kicked the back of Kizzie's chair until the other girl turned around. "What?"

"Who is this?" Angela held up her own copy of the book and pointed at a pencil drawing. "This bloke here. Who is 'e?"

"It's him. Whatsisname. Shakespeare!"

"Seriously?" Angela was wide eyed. "Well, you know what? That's the guy I saw this morning up on The Gallops!"

"What?"

"Swear to God."

"Ladies!"

Angela and Kizzie looked up. "Sorry, miss," they both said.

"What page, Mr Harari?"

"Three, miss."

"Three. That's right. We have lift off. Here we go. Outer space. Sources."

Angela stared down into the eyes of William Shakespeare: they were the same, slightly lost, mildly wild eyes she'd seen on the hill, pencil-grey in the book, blue in real life. And the earring, too. That was the strange thing. *Oh, my God – and the clothes!* Impulsively her hand shot up. "Miss!"

"Yes, Angela? Shock me."

"Is this William Shakespeare, miss?" Angela held up the book.

"It's a likeness of the great man, yes."

"Sure, sure, miss? I mean, like, one hundred percent?"

"It's one of the likenesses that's generally thought to represent Shakespeare, yes, Angela," replied Miss Tartt. How far should she go into this? Just last night she'd been involved in an internet spat with an Oxfordian who believed Shakespeare had not written any of the plays or poems attributed to him.

"So it might not be him?"

"It's him," declared Miss Tartt, with some finality. "Eyes down, let's get on with this, I need a coffee."

"Promise?"

"Angela." The teacher put the book down on her desk and folded her arms. "All right, I'll play. Hit me with it. Why are you so desperate to know?"

"I just," Angela felt the eyes of the class burning into her. Kizzie's seemed to be pleading with her not to tell the truth. "I just really want to know what he looked like, miss."

"Why? We can form a picture of him from his words, Angela," Miss Tartt began, "of which he left us plenty. Besides, it's a futile exercise to try to image exactly how he looked physically as too much time has passed and we could never be quite sure. And then there's the fact that it's not important. What's important are the words, the plays – ah! *The play's the thing* – so it is, so it is. And today we're looking at the sources of the plays, *our* play specifically, aren't we? Yes, the sources. Yes, we are. Which, oh, my dedicated followers of fashion, are described on page?"

"Three," came a chorus of weary voices.

"Mr Keats. Read, if you will. Do your worst, my friend."

"What, miss?"

"The paragraph which is headed, 'sources', sir. Read the goddamn thing."

"Ah, ok, miss."

"Miss Tartt?"

"Gillian. Let's chat! Yes? What's on your mind?"

"May I; could I ask you a question, miss?"

The teacher examined Gillian's face and saw worry writ large. She dropped the act and the two of them stepped outside the classroom, in to the small vestibule where the children waited in bad weather; and a moment later everyone nearest the windows watched Gillian walk away around the corner of the nearest classroom towards The Quad. They dived back into their seats as the teacher re-entered the room.

"Kizzie, take her things if she doesn't come back, please," Miss Tartt said. Then, changing back into character, the teacher took up her book and her position at the front of the class and barked, "Sources! Here we go. Next one to interrupt will be garrotted! Let's go. Where are we? Where were we? Where are we going? What comes after two? What's the atomic number of lithium? How many sons did Noah have? The fourth Fibonacci number and what you get if you say tree with a lisp *is*...?"

Gillian kept up her pained face until she'd walked through The Quad and was going down the steps towards the Main Building. She'd complained of a stomach ache and made sure that anyone peeking out of the windows at her, teacher or student, would be convinced she was in real pain. And, indeed, she was in pain: her entire body felt wracked with a desire to see the boy from the fields again.

She wasn't quite sure how she was going to manage it: she only knew that she'd go up to where the offices were, and see if she could find out what had happened. The Magistrate had taken him and that meant he'd probably be under their guard somewhere inside the Main Building. But after that, what? Would they call the police? Take him away? Gillian's first thought was for the boy's comfort: would they have given him clothes, made sure he'd eaten something? Were they looking after him properly?

The back door was open, the Hall empty but for a healthy fire. Gillian thought about checking the Eleusinian Room but decided against it: she wasn't a prefect and there was no way she'd be able to get in. Her best hope was that the boy might be upstairs and she could pretend she was on her way to her house to get medicine for her stomach.

She climbed the stairs slowly, hunched over, acting again, ready at any moment to explain her presence, but nobody stopped her and when she got to the headmaster's landing she saw no sign of life but for some damp, fading, half-footprints on the green carpet.

He's still up here, she thought, and couldn't help smiling.

Gillian didn't think twice. She began creeping along the landing, careful to avoid the creaking centre, until she was in the small passageway where the Headmaster's study and the Secretary's rooms were. She could hear voice – Firmin, someone else, more teachers – in the Headmaster's study. She pressed her ear to the Secretary's door, heard nothing and on instinct tried the handle. It was locked. She crouched to peep through the keyhole and saw him, the boy, sitting on a chair with the only window in the room bright as a spotlight behind him.

He had a brown blanket thrown around his shoulders and looked drawn and tired. Gillian wanted to call out him and tapped as lightly as she could on the door with her short, square fingernails. She saw him come to life, as though out of a daze, and he came over to the door and crouched down by the keyhole, sniffing like a dog.

"Are you all right?" Gillian whispered. She was so close to the door she could taste the bitter metal of the handle fixture.

"Can you get me out?" the boy's voice came back, also a whisper.

"The door's locked."

"Also, the window." The boy had an accent, she noticed. Not strong but not local nor British. More European. Southern European. Italian?

"Wait. I have an idea." Gillian had thought of something: the girl's trunk room, where they kept their cases and trunks, was next to the Secretary's office. The walls adjoined. Perhaps there was some way she could get from the trunk room into the office? Perhaps there was an old door or a thin piece of wall? "I'll be back in a sec."

"Don't go!"

Gillian back away and straightened up but as she turned down the main corridor she bumped hard into the chest of Alain Verne. "Ouch!"

"Gillian?" Alain picked his phone from the floor. "What're you doing here?"

"I wanted to check on the boy," she said, unable to lie.

Alain's face darkened and he shook his head. "He's not here."

"What? I just saw him."

"You can't see him," Alain replied, growling before he could stop it. He wanted to control himself but raised a hand, a warning finger wagging. "Gillian, you don't know what's happening. That boy is very dangerous. We have a big problem with him." He took a deep breath, looked once at the Headmaster's door and then back to the girl. "Please. You must trust me. I can't tell you any more than this but you must not think of him anymore. Don't even think about contacting him. That boy is not what you think he is. It's something complicated. Something strange.

Unnatural."

Gillian had her wits about her now and nodded. "Fine."

Alain smiled and caught her by the elbow as she turned away. "One more thing."

"What?" Gillian shook herself free. The boy's grip was strong, like a pinch, and had hurt her.

"Did you speak to your friend about me?"

"Who?"

"Kizzie?"

"No."

Alain nodded. "Maybe we can talk some time? I'd like to ask you something."

"Maybe. Not now, you know. Maybe later."

There was a bang from one of the office doors and Alain turned his head. Gillian grabbed her chance and set off in the other direction, towards the house. Frustratingly, the trunk room was locked and after a quick tour of the empty dorms she walked back out into the corridor in time to hear raised voices on the stairs. Leaning out over the banisters she saw the boy – *her boy* – in the centre of a group of prefects and teachers, his head covered with the blanket but his arms and feet bare on the brown stairs.

The people with him were shouting at him and Gillian felt tears spring up in her eyes as she watched. *Stop being so cruel!* she tried to say but her voice was barely a whisper.

As the noisy party reached the Main Hall, the boy flung off the blanket and there was an anxious cry of voices and some violent shouting. The air lit up with tension. Gillian saw the boy's bare shoulders flex and watched as two teachers went sprawling across the wooden floor on their backs, shock on their red faces.

After a moment's wonder, she turned and ran back through to the Dorm, running down the centre of the threadbare carpet to the window and pressing herself against the glass. She was just in time to see the naked boy sprinting away across the lawn chased by Alain, some other male members of the Magistrate and two puffing teachers.

Half-laughing, half-crying, Gillian shouted him on, banging on the glass: "Keep going! Keep going! Keep going!"

9

Angela ran uphill in the dusk behind the pack of glowing, white singlets. The afternoon was so dark and gloomy that some of the leading girls were wearing climber's lights. The beams danced about the tangled roots and bushes and turned the footpath into a tunnel.

This was Angela's second run of the day but she felt fine. She was with the cross-country team, pretending she was training again to keep her stamina up. "I might take the short way back, Oban," Angela told the leader as she slowed and waved the others on.

"Your ankle still sore from this morning, is it?" Oban raised an eyebrow.

"No. Just some twinges here and there. Don't want to do any damage."

"Want me to send Joe or Sophie back with you? They'll go by Alveston or St Gregory's?"

Angela pulled a face. "Nah, I'm fine. I know the way like the back of my hand."

"All right," replied Oban, nodding. "Watch it though. Stay on the path and check in as soon as you get back." He put his hands to his head. "Want to borrow my light?"

"No, no. I'll be quick."

"Careful, then."

Angela nodded her assent and let herself back into the line of runners. It was so dark she couldn't see the brambles tugging and snagging her clothes, only the white flashes of the trainers of the girl in front.

When they came out at the The Gallops, Angela bent to tie a loose lace. She watched Oban, Sophie, Joe and the last of the white bibs fade into the gloom and set off in the opposite direction. The air was cold and clammy, as though there were dead snakes hanging, unseen, from the blotchy boughs. Alone, her breathing seemed louder; alone it always felt like there was someone being you, following you. Angela did what she always did and spoke aloud: *Hello trees. Just look after me. I'm going home, that's all. Just running home.*

She looked up and saw the full moon staring back at her from an empty, grey, bruised sky. It seemed to reveal the path ahead, lighting the way silvery-bright and the small hairs on the nape of Angela's neck prickled.

The birds were singing a song that they only ever sang at sundown, pretty but sad. The noise always reminded her of her first night at St Francis, homesick and lost, lying on a scratchy blanket in her dorm, sleep and home a million miles away. If things were bad now, how had they been for the fat little girl who'd turned up at St Francis's four years ago?

Were things really better now? Angela wasn't sure. When she'd been fat, ugly and weird at least she'd been left alone. Now she had no way of avoiding people. She had to show this horrendous mess of a face to everyone, never mind how she woke up in the morning. It was humiliating, soul-destroying, to watch people's eyes widen as they examined the eruptions and stains on her face, inclining their heads pityingly and thinking, so clearly Angela could hear it, *oh, you poor thing, looking like that.*

And she did look horrible, there was no point pretending otherwise. She looked a mess. Foul! Even her hair, no matter how many times she washed it, was constantly greasy. Her skin looked like someone had wiped an oily cloth over it. Her forehead seemed to be smeared with smashed up strawberry, and spattered with yellow paint. She was horrendous!

Can I have a piece of your face for dinner?

Oh God.

Running was the only thing these days that made her feel better. Maybe if she kept running she'd get away from it all? From herself? Just keep running and never have to come back.

Come back and be someone else! Why did everyone else – and, yes, it was everyone in the whole school, in her whole life – have better skin than her? Normal ears? Normal chins, thighs, ankles, shoulders and no weird scraggy necks and bad nails? Why was it everyone else had something that was more or less all right? Because normally, in this situation, people thought, *well, at least you're not so and so*. But she *was* so and so! She was the worst case scenario. She was as bad as it gets and there was no way of ignoring that.

I'm the bottom of the ladder.

The light that had been guiding her faded in a blink and Angela stumbled on a root, almost falling, and threw out her hands, the soles of her shoes slapping in the mud.

It was intensely, suddenly cold. Like stepping into a freezer.

Angela collided with something solid, soft and immovable. She bounced off it, hearing a male voice say – "I beg your pardon" – and became airborne, landing heavily on her backside and ended up sitting like a toddler, legs apart, back straight, hands held up in front of her face. She was even drooling.

Her hands, turned this way and that in the moonlight breaking from the clouds, were coated in thick, brown, icy mud. She saw a man dead ahead, also knocked onto his backside, sitting across the path, looking dazed and bemused. And there they were: those eyes again. Staring eyes; a sea of white around the dark, blue yolks. He had a high forehead. The earring, too. Balding, startled but friendly: all like the picture in the book.

"Who are you?" Angela asked. She was half up on her palms and the balls of her feet, ready to flee.

"I only want the school," the man replied, lifting a dirty hand. He had an accent; sounded like a farmer.

"Which school?" Angela stood and the two circled each other slowly. The moon was slipping away again, being smothered.

"The school." He put one hand up and turned from the waist, like an actor on the stage. "The school I know is hereabouts."

Hereabouts? "Who are you? Why are you dressed like that? So...*weird?*"

The man was wearing big leather boots and his pants fluffed up over the tops of them at his thighs. His fingernails were black as night, rimed with dirt. When he spoke, Angela noticed his teeth: uneven, sparse and inky. "I might ask you the same question, my girl."

The man's face seemed to fade away and no matter how hard she stared, Angela could only see his clothes: no nose, no eyes, no hands, and no neck. But then he spoke, from a space where she could see dark boughs hanging leafless in the air. "If you would be so kind as to show me the way to the school, I would be much obliged."

Angela backed away from the strange, headless figure without saying a word.

"Don't go, miss!"

Angela scrabbled through the scrub, banging her head on low branches and clawing at bracken until she'd made it diagonally up the hill to the path she'd been on. Without looking back, her breath heavy and laboured, she ran home along a Gallop's path occasionally lit by temperamental moonlight.

Only when she got to the school, the lights at the main entrance glowing with dim orange halos, did she stagger to a halt. Right on cue she saw the bobbing, flickering lights of the cross-country club coming down the main road from St Catherine's and the *Admiral Benbow*.

"Oh thank god for that," she said, the sweat on her forehead making her acne sting.

Tuesday

1

It was the middle of the night and Gillian was wide awake.

The middle of the night might have been the middle of the ocean. She was in the middle of nowhere, the full moon hanging high ahead of her through the gap in the curtains, staring back at her with its dark, uneven eye. It was dead, floating, circling the earth, pulling the tides, stirring up the oceans, dividing the year, being howled at and stared at and wished upon, ignored and cursed.

Tick.

Gillian had tried all of her usual tricks but was still awake. It was as though someone had turned a radio on in her head. Thoughts were playing; music too: a song she hadn't heard for months. A slow song. A love song. A sad song. A song she hated that everyone was singing: why was it always the awful, cheesy ones you couldn't get out of your head?

She tried turning around in bed but her body was tired of the same troughs in the mattress and folds in the sheets. The more she thought about sleeping, the more awake she felt. Then came quiet desperation: she knew that she was going to be tired the next day, dropping off in class, in a bad mood with everyone, probably suffering one of those headaches that made you want to unzip your skin and step out of your body.

Tick.

This was not going to be funny in the morning.

Tick.

What?

The intermittent noises were coming from the window and the explanation that made the most sense to Gillian was that the old panes were creaking due to changes in the temperature. It was the coldest part of the night now, deepest night. Clear, cold and empty.

Normally I sleep through this. This is something normal. It's completely normal.

Gillian slipped out of bed with practised ease. She could hear one of the other girls sighing, dreaming, and see the bundle of shadows which was Kizzie.

At the window she looked down through the gap in the curtains at the playing fields and back lawns lit up by the moon and thought how different everything looked at night. The school swimming pool, a covered over, seemingly bottomless, square, looked terrifying, like a portal to hell. Yet in summer it was full of screaming, merry children, the very definition of fun.

A portal to hell. Gillian couldn't help smiling at her own words as she checked the handle. *Huh. Someone's happy.*

Looking out, she thought of the boy and stared through her dark reflection in the glass, out at the wooded hills, at the cold night, and hoped he was all right, wherever he was. *Oh, why you?* she thought. *Why now? Why here? Why can't I ever do anything properly? Why does everything have to be so complicated?*

Why couldn't they simply have met that night when she was on holiday, perhaps talked, perhaps kissed? Everything could have been normal. They could have gone swimming together, gone for walks, maybe sailing. They could have eaten meals together, sworn undying love; promised to always remember each other when they looked up at the stars or the moon. They could have made each other happy the usual way. The right way.

They might even have kept in touch. They might have visited each other.

She might have gone back to Italy to see him and they might have ridden around sunny plazas on mopeds and eaten fast-melting ice creams by the fountains they were dipping their feet into. He might have taken her to visit his family somewhere up in hazy hills covered with stumpy, smelly olive trees, brittle with heat. His mother would have loved her because Gillian would have radiated charm.

Hmm. He might have had older brothers, too.

Or, or, he might have come home with her and they could have gone for walks along the coast at home. Or she could have taken him to Inverness and they could have spent a week hunting Nessie in a log cabin high above the loch. Or just spent a week in a log cabin high above the loch. He would have met and charmed her parents and…and…

Maybe not.

Tick.

This time Gillian saw the cause of the noise. A tiny pebble, no more than a slither of rock, collided with the window pane right in front of her nose. It left a small, dusty mark.

Tick.

Now another. And she knew it was him. That same sixth sense she'd felt before, which arrived accompanied by a small surge of joy and pleasure which coursed through her body, told her it was true. It was the feeling that everything was all right, that for once the stars were aligned, that for once things were going to go her way.

Gillian opened the old jamb carefully to avoid the squeak and let herself out through the small gap which filled with icy, inrushing night.

Sometimes in summer, at the weekends, when the school was quiet, the girls sneaked out onto this small, tarmac-covered balcony to sunbathe. Now it was soaked with the milky glow of moonlight and Gillian crouched by its edge.

"Hello again."

Down in the darkness a figure formed. It was him, the boy, beautifully handsome and quite magical. Gillian felt her face pulled in odd contortions: she was smiling, a natural movement, and it almost hurt. "What are you doing here?"

"I had to see you."

He was wearing clothes, she was glad to see, beaming up at her, happy to hear in her tone, if not her words, that she was pleased to see him. Gillian couldn't help remembering what Alain Verne had told her outside the office and hissed down at him, "How did you get here? I want some answers!"

"I don't know," came the accented reply, delicate and cute. The boy was grinning, arms out from his sides, shrugging, bottom lip pushed out. He looked as though he genuinely didn't know but, at the same time, genuinely didn't care.

"Well, where do you come from, then? Can't you tell me anything?"

"I remember driving," he replied thoughtfully, dancing with her eyes. "It was a normal night, coming home from a party. I was with my motorcycle. And then I remember nothing. Here. I remember waking up here, over there." He pointed into the darkness.

"The playing fields? Where we found you?"

"Yes, yes. Football."

"What's your name?"

The boy was about to speak, thought better of it, looked around at where he was, looked up to where she was, and winked. "Call me Romeo, no? I think it's perfect."

"What?"

"And you? What? Julia? Juliet?"

"Gillian. Near enough, I guess." She put her hands on the low brick wall. *Romeo and Gillian. Oh lordy.* "This is my balcony then, is it?"

"Gillian." *Jee-Lee-Anne.*

"Are you real?"

"Real?"

Gillian thought he hadn't heard her and became impatient. "Oh, I'm gonna come down there. This is ridiculous."

The boy – Romeo, for that's what he wanted to be called – quickly took in the situation. "No, no, no. Wait, wait!"

Gillian, chest against the low wall, watched him disappear. He seemed to be swallowed up by the night, a crow drowning in ink, and she blinked and stared but couldn't see where he'd gone. Immediately she thought she'd imagined the whole thing but knew she hadn't. But the night was persuasive. Gradually its insistent enveloping of her senses, its vastness and its creeping chill made her pull her dressing gown lapels closed and think of going back inside.

"Mind if I join you?" Romeo hopped over the wall and landed softly beside her. "I like your slippers."

"I like your duffel coat."

Face-to-face, eye-to-eye again, they became nervous. They sat side by side with their backs against the wall looking at the closed windows, the backs of the ugly dorm curtains, the redbrick wall, the roof and stars, in a weird silence. Despite all their eyes had told each other and the sheer unlikelihood of ever meeting again, both were paralysed.

"Are you going to tell me where you're really from?"

"I told you, I don't know."

"But you are real, right? I mean – you exist?"

"Touch me." He held up his hand and she took it. "Feel me. You can feel me, can't you?"

"I'm scared that you're not real."

"But I'm here. Feel me! I'm here."

"Yes, but –" Gillian looked up at the sky – "look at the stars. Their light is here but they're dead, aren't they? It takes so long for their light to get here it's not really them we see, is it? Or, or look at the moon. The moon's here but it's dead, too, isn't it? It's there, yes. It affects us. It's real but it's dead. It's a stone, that's all. Without the sun it wouldn't shine. Wouldn't live." Her thoughts and voice trailed off. "Oh, I don't know what I'm trying to say."

"Don't compare me to the moon," the boy replied, keeping hold of her hand. "It's too far away, it changes too much. I'm not. You know I'm not." He waited for her to turn her head. "I don't change. I'm here now. I don't know how. I don't even know why. I only know what I feel. Why I had to come. And that's you, Gillian. Only because of you. Since I saw you, I don't know, this makes sense. I am here because of you. Because of this. It's the only thing that seems to make the whole thing make sense."

"How did you get away from them before?" Gillian had her head in her hands and had been groaning. "How did you climb up here? This is crazy. It's impossible. You're not real!"

"I did it because I love you. That's all I can say."

"They're going to kill you if they find you here."

"Kiss me and I'll die happy."

"No, really. I'm serious." She stared at him as seriously and as coldly as she could, hoping, in some part of her, that he would disappear. "You really shouldn't be here."

"There's nowhere I can go."

"How did you even know I was here? In this dorm? This very dorm, I mean."

The boy laughed and it was beautiful. He laughed in a carefree way, a true way, which Gillian felt, even as she fought to keep a straight face, lift her own soul. "I don't know. I wanted to find you. I knew you were here. I can feel you before I see you."

"I don't know what to do."

"Do you love me?"

"Are you serious?"

"You do."

"What you are saying?"

Gillian's true self, which she kept hidden, divided in pieces between her heart and soul, protected by witty words, behind a shield of answers, routines and diversions, briefly surfaced in her eyes. She was terrified and looked it. It was the most precious thing she had and she kept it well guarded.

Romeo saw it and his own face changed: they were like two flames flickering alongside each other, blown by the same breath. "I swear I love you. I swear by..." He looked around. "Just look at me and tell me you do. You don't have to swear by anything. Just tell me the truth."

"I do! I do! I do!" Gillian felt a brief moment of ecstasy, of fulfilment, but then all her insecurities, past hurts and worries, and her instinct to withdraw and take care of herself, returned. "Oh, this is too fast. Too stupid. What am I thinking?"

He watched her stand up in her dressing gown and smiled at how much he loved her. "Where are you going?"

"I can't do this!"

He took the crook of her arm, standing in front of her, not letting her go. "You're going to leave me now, no? Like this?"

"What do you want?" Another Gillian appeared and with her the ball of anger and fire which had kept her alive so long, which burned around her innermost self, protecting she and her secrets as a dragon does its treasure. "What do you want from me?"

"I want you to marry me."

"What?" Gillian couldn't help thinking: *Kizzie could do it. She's always going on about it. Her magic stuff. Her spells. Her hippie stuff.*

"Say you love me!"

Gillian turned at a light from the window. "Oh, no, this is too much. No. I have to go. You have to go. Go!"

In the time it took Kizzie to open the window – to a squeak like a mandrake's scream – Romeo had vanished.

"What the hell are you doing out here, Gil?" Kizzie asked, her eyes swollen with sleep.

"Nothing," replied Gillian, rubbing her cold neck. "Thinking. Couldn't sleep."

"You're nuts. It's freezing. Come inside."

"I know, I know."

Gillian climbed into bed and lay waiting for Kizzie to come back from the toilet, the other girl's creaking footfalls creaking back along the old corridor as the clanking flush dissolved. The others stirred as Kizzie settled, turning once or twice, but finally there was a moment of complete silence followed by the beginnings of a steady snoring rhythm from Kizzie's bunk. Gillian counted to one hundred as slowly as she could and eased herself out of bed. She turned the handle in the special way and stepped back out onto the balcony.

In a hoarse, strong whisper, she called, "Hey!" It must have been three now. The school grounds were dead silent. Even the moon was covered up and dozing. "Romeo!"

From the gloom came a sound and Gillian made out a shadow. "Here!"

Do it, she told herself. The only thing she'd been able to think in bed, the only true thought she'd had, was that she *must* see him again. Despite not knowing who he was, how he'd got there or what was going on, she had to see him again. "Let's meet tomorrow."

"What time?"

Gillian sighed, her hands on the low wall, which felt like a shelf of ice. This was a fantastic dream, a special one all right. "Eight."

"Where?"

"The Dips. Do you know it?"

"No."

Gillian shook her head in frustration. *Of course he didn't.* "The tennis courts? The farthest wall? Near the road? There are two trees there, old trees? Sycamores? Their branches make a kind of roof?"

"I will find it."

"At eight!"

"Eight!"

"If you're not there I'll kill you!"

"It's a deal! Go to sleep!"

Gillian backed away, smiling, lifting the hinge, stepping over the threshold and getting back into bed. She lay with her hands clasped on her chest in a knot. Her heart was thumping like a rave and she felt that if she smiled any wider she might split her face apart.

She was still in her dressing gown and didn't care.

She was still in her slippers and didn't care.

She didn't care about anything anymore.

She was happy.

2

Just over four hundred years to the day earlier, a snorting mule hauled a cartload of dead bodies up a frosty hill and a well-wrapped traveller stepped aside as blackened fingers wagged at him. Another cart, driven by a toothless man with his head bowed and his collar drawn up over his nose, came lurching up the black ice behind the first. It, too, was laden with corpses: gaunt cheeks and pecked-out eyes filling up with falling snow.

The traveller stumbled backwards into a ditch. The black water was frozen but gave way and chilly juice soaked him to the ankle. He sucked himself out and trudged away across the frosted, ploughed fields. Anywhere but the road. Anything but the plague.

A night's solid walking brought the traveller to the grounds of a ruined abbey. There was a flickering light in a wattle and daub outhouse whose windows glowed like tigers' eyes. As he trudged up to the door, his bandaged feet numb, the traveller heard chickens clucking. The hatch snapped open at eye-height and a woman with a throbbing boil right between her eyes barked, "Well? What is it? Whaddya want at this time-a night?"

"I'm looking for work, ma'am," the traveller answered, hat in hand. "I'm a schoolmaster but I'd take any odd jobs for grub right now. 'Til the worst of the weather passes, anyhows."

"Don't need no schoolmasters 'ere," came the reply. The traveller heard pigs at the woman's back; pigs and snorting horses. He smelled dung and straw. The crone blinked furiously. "Don't need anyone 'ere as a matter-a fact."

"I see." The traveller braced himself and asked the old lady if he might shelter somewhere on the grounds for the night. "Seeing as it's so cold and that, out."

She wiped her long, dripping nose on a dirty sleeve. "Not an inn, either." But a raised palm indicated he should wait.

The hatch slammed shut and the traveller took in his surroundings, blowing into his hands to warm them. Directly in front of the Main Building was a flat, uneven meadow spotted with dollops of manure. A night mist was coming in, oozing from between the trunks, which lined the entrance path, filling the open spaces. The full moon was gradually being rubbed out by cloud and the traveller thought of his wife and young children. If it wasn't for them he'd have stopped long ago: lain down to sleep and die in some frozen field in the middle of nowhere.

A male voice not more than a whisper sounded over his shoulder, "Come inside, then, my friend. Don't dawdle. Come inside, out of the cold."

The traveller wheeled about: the wooden door was open, golden warmth within, and he saw the ground floor was indeed a shuffling menagerie of animals. An elderly, cowled, shrivelled monk with misty-blue marbles for eyes, took the traveller's hands in his own. "Come on inside, my boy, come on inside. Follow me in, follow me in. There's a fire over here, look. Get yourself warm, won't you? 'Tis bitter cold out there, I'll bet."

"God bless you, kind sir."

"Travelled far, have you, my young friend?" The two men stood together amid the snuffling pigs. The monk was trembling in hands and lips.

"A fair distance, sir, yes. From the Midlands, sir, or thereabouts."

"Oh! Quite a journey, then." The monk licked his lips to wet them and whistled his s's. "The Midlands. I see. I see. And what brings you here, of all places, if I may be so impertinent as to enquire?"

"I'm bound for London, sir, but, perhaps now is not the best time to be in the city."

"Plague, again, eh?"

"I believe so, sir." The traveller saw those blackened, wagging fingers again, banging up and down to the rhythm of the cart.

"Schoolmaster, are we?" The monk nodded his trembling head at the traveller's satchel. "Mrs Sharpe said something about you being a learned man. Came here looking for work, I suppose? The villagers at the *Benbow* pointed you here, did they? Yes, well. We're trying to make a go of it. One must stay true to one's principles, eh? Follow one's own convictions. Do what's right, as it were."

The traveller thought the monk might be nervous. Religion was a sensitive political subject. "I only wish shelter for the night, sir. I wish to cause no trouble. If there is work, sir, I should be happy to undertake it. If not I shall be on my way at dawn."

"Yes, yes. Very well. I see. You may sleep here, of course." The old monk wafted a hand around the clucking, snivelling beasts. Two pigs were standing beneath the traveller, dirty ears bent over their black snouts, sniffing and licking at the mud, or whatever it was they liked, on his boots. "They'll all settle down shortly, I shouldn't wonder. They'll need their sleep too."

The traveller looked around the dirty floor and walls. There was a small hay shelf which looked sturdy enough and he thought he might sleep there. Anything was better than another night outside. "I shall be more than comfortable here, sir. And I thank you and your lady for your hospitality."

The monk bowed and then began to haul himself up a leaning ladder to the upper floor, his sandals raining dust from the wooden rungs. "Mrs Sharpe will bring you supper shortly," the monk called down. "I'm sure you could use something to eat and drink."

"Many thanks again, sir. Most kind of you."

But when Mrs Sharpe did come down the ladder, wart bulging, in a foul temper, carrying a tray of bread, cheese and small beer, she found the young man snoring on the hay shelf as the pigs made light work of his satchel.

3

Alain Verne was in the bathtub in the attic of the Old Cottage, his head propped up against the white rim of the tub. He was sweating, the water scalding hot, a flannel draped across his reddening chest. He had read that Napoleon took baths like this and Napoleon was fast becoming a hero of his. It wasn't because he was French but because he was his own man. Self-made. Fearless.

OK – French too. That didn't hurt.

A bath, one's own private bathroom, was a privilege which came to Alain as Head of the Magistrate. The room itself was only small, the antiquated toilet jammed up against the edge of the tub, the cistern bubbling by the roof and the roof itself so angular and sloping so steeply that you had to mind your head not to bang it, but it was *his*. Only his. No shared showers or urinals for Alain!

The wind blew against the window in gusts. Alain closed his eyes, disregarded the infrequent thumps, the leaking tap and the water dripping off his nose into the water and thought of Gillian.

She was his default setting, the Queen of his mind. She was there when he closed his eyes and he studied her as a though she were a piece of art, which she was. He watched her now, sighing to himself, wondering how something so wonderful could ever have been created. As she revolved slowly in the darkness of his mind he saw her lovely, kissable mouth open and heard her whisper, *"Beware water."*

The Head of the Magistrate opened his eyes. *"Qui est là?"*

There was a scratching on the door of the bathroom and the single bulb above the sink flickered. Something was pressing against the door. Scratching. Whining.

"Who's there?" Alain sat up in the steaming water and some slopped out over the edge onto the tiles, landing with a splat. He swore. "I'm in the bath! Get out!"

The door was pushed slowly open and a large male baboon padded in on all fours. Its face was bright red and blue, its mane grey, furry and fluffed up. Behind its sleek, swishing, muscular body, its tail was up, waving too. Its small, dark eyes fixed on Alain and it came to an unhurried halt before him baring its teeth in a terrible, silent scream.

Alain was frozen, one knee out of the water. He could smell the animal.

The bulb flickered and died and he was cast into darkness. He could hear the baboon breathing. Hear its nails scratching on the tiles.

Good evening, a voice told him.

Alain was wide awake now, blind, completely blind, but aware of movement. Coolness replaced the stench of beast. Cold rushed in around him. He felt as though he were floating. He was not in his bathroom. Looking down, he couldn't see himself. No water. "Who are you?"

I confirm your suspicions.

"Master?"

It is I.

"My suspicions?"

In the vast, inky murk, which comprised his field of vision, Alain thought he could make out a lighter area somewhere up above him, where the sloping ceiling should have been. Perhaps this was the ceiling or a glimpse at whatever form the Master had taken. But then the dark floor lightened, too, and he had a sensation of moving upwards, of rising towards the higher light.

The imposter is not real.

"The boy?" Alain gasped. "I knew it!"

Indeed.

"Is he here?" Alain looked about him. "Here in the school, I mean? Is he still here?"

Of course. He cannot escape.

"And you can't find him? I thought you had people for that? I thought that's what you did?"

The Master remained silent.

"I apologise," Alain muttered, blind eyes staring about the darkness. "I'm sorry, I didn't mean to be rude. I'm just worried. If one of them is here, I need to know. I need to sort things out. Can you take me back? I don't even know where I am! Am I dreaming? Take me back now and I will find the boy. I will find him and remove him!"

You are in water.

Alain looked up. Yes, through that shimmering, wobbling ceiling of light above him he could see clouds and trees, like reflections. Like looking up through the surface of water.

Beware water.

Alain felt cold liquid fill his mouth, ears and nostrils and knew he would drown if he didn't swim upwards immediately. The chill liquid tasted of mud and grit got between his teeth. He kicked blind. Kicked on. Closing his stinging eyes, he broke the surface, feeling daylight and wind. He gulped air.

A cold morning. Rocks, sharp against his hands, water black at his neck like a too-tight collar.

He was tiny, minute. The wind fierce. Plants wild and flapping like tongues.

Staring ahead at the vast gravel horizon Alain saw an enormous ant stop and block out the sun. It twitched its black, shiny head and Alain thought about diving underwater to escape it but then both of them noticed a growing rumbling, like far off thunder, and the ant scuttled away.

"Oh, no."

Alain dragged himself out of the puddle using a twig the size of a branch floating near his head. Heaving himself out, he ran for the grass verge as a herd of white trainers came beating down the path. Gigantic waves doused him and the backwash unbalanced him. Only by jamming himself across the bars of the grate, body rigid, star-shaped, did he manage to avoid being sucked down the drain.

When the waters subsided, cascading away to the well-bottom sewer, he crawled to his feet, sodden, and balanced his way across one of the iron beams like a gymnast. He negotiated the tarmac, scaled the kerb and ran into St Nicholas House under the back door.

A moment later he was normal size, standing, dripping, in his bathroom in the Old Cottage, the light bulb flickering and holding, paw marks on the tiles and a voice in his head, but not his own, repeating, each time more softly than the last:

Beware water.

Beware water.

Beware water.

4

"Kizzie...Kizzie!"

A scything wind was sharpening the thorns on the rose bushes which lined the route of the girls' morning run. While the boys made their circuit clad only in shorts and trainers, the girls ran in jumpers, cardigans, tracksuits and, sometimes, with duvets wrapped around their shoulders.

Kizzie's fair complexion was stained strawberry from the exertion of running against the wind. She jogged on the spot as her friend ran up. "Gil? What's up? Are you all right, babes?"

"Aye, why?"

"Because normally you don't say a word until after breakfast."

Gillian managed a smile, panting now that she'd caught Kizzie up. "Come on. Keep going. I need a favour, Kiz. A big favour."

Both girls slowed – eyes flicking housewards to check neither Magistrates nor Miss Bainbridge were on the prowl – and Kizzie, sensing the seriousness in Gillian's expression, inquired after more information. "Go on then." She smiled sympathetically, sniffing through her bright pink nose. "What is it?"

"I wanna get married," Gillian said. "No. Change that. I'm *going* to get married. Aye, I'm going to get married. This morning. And I want you to do it. The ceremony, that is."

Kizzie's face contorted. "*Eh?*"

"I know."

"Rewind."

"I know. I know."

"Married, you say?"

"Aye."

"Who to?"

"Him."

"Who?"

"Him!"

"Alain Verne?"

"What? No!" Now it was Gillian's turn to look horrified. "No, Kizzie, no! Come on!"

"Then who?"

"The guy I was telling you about. The guy from the holiday."

"Oh! *Him.*"

"Yes!"

They jogged on. "Did he message you or something? Track you down online?"

"No!" Gillian shook her arms in exasperation. "It's him, Kiz! The one who was here!"

"Who? Where?"

"From the fields, yesterday."

"The one you kissed?"

"Yes!"

"The naked one?"

"Yes!"

"Bloke from Italy?"

"Yes!"

"Why was he naked?" Kizzie grabbed Gillian. "Oh, did he sell all of his clothes to get here?"

"I don't know!" Gillian pulled her friend close, interlocking elbows. "Look, it doesn't matter what you think, anyway, because it's all sorted. And I know it sounds crazy and I know it sounds nuts but we've talked about it and we don't have much time and we both want to do it."

"Get married. Right." Kizzie's eyelids fluttered closed as a piercing arrow of pure Arctic breath blew through her.

"Aye."

"Oh God, you want me to marry you, don't you?"

"Yes! Come on. You said it. You said it was just a ceremony. You said there were ways. All that stuff, that witchcraft, pagan stuff or whatever. Your books!"

"*Stuff*?"

They were coming close to the entrance. Warmth. Company.

"Will you do it or not?"

"Of course!"

"I love you."

"Love you too, babes!"

"Forever!"

"Whatever."

The sky cleared, the wind dropped and sleet showers stopped and started.

Back in the dorm, Kizzie and Gillian recruited Athy, half-asleep, as maid of honour, and Angela, setting out for a run, said she'd drop off a message to Zak in the boys' House on her way out. "We have to do this right now, do we?" Kizzie asked, looking out of the window.

"Yep, has to be now." Gillian checked her watch.

"I don't get this at all," muttered Athy. She was wearing a multi-coloured, knitted balaclava with matching gloves and was trying to scratch her nose. She ended up having to ask her sister to do it.

"Let's go," said Gillian, anxious, holding open the door.

"Where?" asked Kizzie, scooping bits and pieces from a drawer into the pockets of her coat. "St Catherine's?"

"The Dips."

"Romantic!" Kizzie laughed.

"Just don't say anything," Gillian replied. "To anyone."

The three girls tried their best not to look conspicuous as they filed out of the dorm and walked down a corridor swarming with girls with combs and headphones and tablets and towels, criss-crossing from room to room. Amazingly no one asked where they were going and they used the back stairs to wind their way down to the ground floor where the canteen was steamed up. "Early aren'tcha?" asked one of the kitchen staff, smoking outside the library.

"Quick constitutional," Gillian said, mimicking her grandmother. "Work up an appetite, you know."

"Good luck, lass. Rather you than me."

The girls walked, heads down, through flurries to The Steps and then cut down between the sixth form block and the tennis courts. There was no one about, only the sound of Bob Dylan's *Time Out Of Mind* being played at top volume in the senior boy's house.

The rough scrubland, which led down to The Dips, was hard with hoary frost but mushy in places and they had to be careful. When they got to the stamped-down ground under the kissing sycamores all three exchanged a glance.

"Here?" asked Kizzie.

"Here," nodded Gillian, peeping back the way they'd come.

The sky was eraser white, the snow like the broken shards which are swept off paper. The girls went into a heightened sense of alertness, careful to watch for any approaching movement. Like the roar of a far-off waterfall, the morning traffic on the bypass hummed by behind the old, red-brick wall at their backs.

"And what the devil are you three doing here?"

Gillian screamed and slapped Zak as he bundled in amongst them laughing.

"Idiot!"

"Good soldiers you lot would be!" Zak laughed.

"What are you doing here?" Athena asked quietly. "I seriously don't know what's going on at all. The world's gone mad."

"You sound like gran," laughed Kizzie.

"Hello," Gillian said, suddenly, quietly, in a voice which drew all their attention to the boy who was standing behind them. Even Zak fell silent for a moment. "These are my friends," Gillian explained, introducing the others. "Guys, this is Romeo."

Zak snorted but not for long. "You actually look like a Romeo," he said, shaking the pale boy's hand. "Nice to see you with some clothes on, too, mate."

Romeo laughed. "Sorry you had to see that."

Zak began to mumble something about cold streams and running when, thankfully, he was interrupted.

"Ah!" Athena cried, brightening. "Was that you? Yesterday? Purple?"

"Kiz, can we just get started," Gillian asked. "Just do whatever you have to do."

"What are we doing?" asked Zak and Athena at the same time.

"Us two are going to get married," Gillian explained. "Kizzie's going to do it. You're witnesses."

"What?" asked Athy, shaking her balaclava and lifting her gloves.

"Love it," nodded Zak.

"OK, here's what we're going to do," began Kizzie. She'd tied some manner of tingling, jingling string to the boughs of both trees and as she spoke, she moved everyone into position, Athy behind Romeo and Zak behind Gillian. Kizzie took her place in front of the nervous couple and smiled at them, making them hold hands.

Kizzy began, icy smoke streaming from her lips. "We are gathered here this morning to celebrate a union." Her eyes were honest and clear. "A union of hearts and souls, the hearts and souls of Romeo and Gillian."

Zak made a clicking noise. "Hear, hear."

"Sshh."

"Are we pretending or is this real?" asked Athy.

"We don't have much time so I'm going to keep this short," Kizzie went on. "First I'm going to say that I only agreed to do this for both of you this morning because I believe you are both sincere.

"I know that your love exists because I see it in your eyes.

"Of course, we don't have to make declarations in front of

people, or hold ceremonies, to make a relationship real but I know there is something in you both that wants to. You both want to show us, and show the world, that you are serious about your love and your commitment to each other, and I feel it. I'm honoured I can help."

"Thanks, Kiz," Gillian whispered.

"I believe you both and I'm happy to bear witness to your love," Kizzie continued. "I have no special power vested in me except that I believe I may act, this morning, as the eyes of the world watching you make your vows.

"I ask nature, the universe, and all that has been created to witness what you are saying to each other and what you are promising each other this morning.

"I ask you, too, to be aware of what you are promising the universe, nature, and yourselves.

"As honest as you both are, so your love will be."

"I promise," said Gillian quietly, although nobody had prompted her.

"I promise," added Romeo. He smiled at Gillian and squeezed her hand.

"Zak and Athy, you are here as human eyes, to witness what these two are saying and promising to each other. Do you understand that?"

"I do," each answered in turn.

"Gill and Romeo. What you two are promising is to love each other. To believe that this love you have now, if nurtured and protected and looked after as you would look after yourselves and your own hearts, will carry you both safely across the stormy sea of life." As they nodded, Kizzie took two acorns from her pocket.

"Although your love is strong and bright right now, it is young. I give you these acorns that you may have one each, that you may plant these seeds and watch them grow, two separate things; that you may watch them grow up to be like these trees which shelter us here today, which form our temple, your wedding ground; who also witness your love. Your love will need care, like these seeds. It will need to survive storms, sun, rain, wind and those moments when you simply cannot be there for it. It will need protection.

"Do you both understand?"

Smiling at each other, they said, "We do."

"You came as two people but you will leave as one and now live as one." Kizzie drew a line in the reddish mud at their feet with a branch. "When you step over this line you leave your past behind. You will never be alone. You will always be together."

"Can we jump?" Romeo asked, making Gillian laugh.

"Let's jump," Gillian answered, and they did, hopping together over the line in the dirt and collapsing into each other's arms on the other side.

"Kiss!" shouted Zak, and the happy couple kissed, moving out into the falling rain without noticing they were no longer under the sycamores; without noticing the dark, long-coated figure of Alain Verne standing in front of the sixth-form block.

5

The traveller woke at first light with a chicken on his chest. He scuffed her off and sat up, noticing immediately the remains of his satchel and pieces of chewed up work all over the sawdust floor. "Oh, nay, nay, nay!" As if guilty, the pigs scuttled away from his boots and honked out through the bottom half of the open door. Outside a cockerel crowed. The room smelled of old smoke.

The traveller did his best to gather up the scraps of paper but most of it was gone: either chewed up and digesting in a pig's belly or cartwheeling across the frosty ridges of the allotments outside. What could he do? The traveller noticed Mrs Sharpe's tray from the night before on a shelf in the wall and hungrily, artlessly, ate the hard bread and waxy cheese. His gums hurt and his body felt weak but he forced the food into his stomach, washing it down with the mug of cold, flat beer.

There didn't seem to be anyone in the house and he followed the chickens and ducks outside, pushing open the swinging top-half of the door and stretching in the meek, winter sunlight. The sky was an oddly blank canvas. It might snow or it might clear up, it was difficult to say. The traveller could smell the freshness of the air and liked the place. He had slept well for the first time since leaving home. It was only the second night he'd slept with a real roof over his head. And no bad dreams!

Strolling around the outside of the monk's house, he took in the almost-romantic ruins of the abbey, broken down and grey-blue, stubbled and overgrown. The rafters had long gone but two of the great walls remained almost intact. Pigeons and starlings poked and fussed from holes in the masonry while a cat licked its lips and prowled below. There was part of a tower nearby: he noticed the smoke snaking up from its wooden roof but mistook it for a cloud and was distracted by a cry from out on the open land.

"Hi! Hi!"

The traveller put his hand to his brow and looked out over the empty green heath. A stocky figure was standing silhouetted by the sun, arms out as though crucified, and the traveller thought it was the figure a scarecrow until it moved and called out again.

"Hi!"

It seemed natural to the young man to walk closer and see what was going on. A few chickens followed him as far as the first fence and a mongrel with patches of pink skin broke off scratching long enough to bark at him and snap at his ankles, but Will paid him no mind. At the sewage ditch, he held his nose and leapt across to the far bank and the figure in the field turned at the thud on the turf. The traveller saw it was Mrs Sharpe.

"May I approach?" he called out, steam billowing from his cupped hands.

"If ye must."

"If ye must," the traveller repeated, walking over. *Yea, I must!*

Mrs Sharpe lifted her arm and cried again, "Hi, hi!"

The young man ducked as a noisy shape flew in close behind his ear. Opening his eyes and coming out of the crouch, he saw a gorgeous beige bird of prey on Mrs Sharpe's arm. "A falcon, ma'am?" The bird twitched its head, its yellow eyes examining the traveller.

For the first time the old lady softened. "He likes birds?"

"He does," nodded the traveller, approaching to examine the falcon as it tore at a strip of flesh Mrs Sharp held in her gnarly fingers. "Ah, she's a beauty."

"That she is," Mrs Sharpe replied proudly. But she took the meat from the talons and shook her head, tutting to the bird. "No, no, Bess. We don't want ye fed up, now, do we? We want ye hungry and keen."

"Bess?" asked the traveller.

"Bess." Mrs Sharpe turned, lifted her arm, made some almost

imperceptible movement and the falcon took flight, batting its gorgeous wings and rising high into the empty sky. "And you?"

"Me, ma'am?"

"Who might you be?"

"Will," the traveller answered.

"Will of the Midlands, eh?"

"Will of Stratford. Will Shakespeare, it is."

"Very grand, I'm sure."

"Oh, I don't think so."

After a pause to check on Bess – a swerving line of black – and without looking back, Mrs Sharpe asked, "And is he married?"

"He is."

"With children?"

"He is."

"Then why is he here?"

"To make his fortune," came the reply. "To see the world. To go to London. For we only have so much time, do we not? None to waste, that's for sure."

"He's ambitious!" Mrs Sharpe forced herself to laugh scornfully.

"He is."

"Then he would not be satisfied being a schoolmaster here, methinks."

"Why not?"

Mrs Sharpe looked at Will and made herself laugh so hard she started coughing. "What is it ye occupy yourself with? What were those scraps I saw this morning flying about? Poetry is it?"

Something about the woman's affront, her obvious need to denigrate him, made Will's pride prickle, and he decided he would stand up for himself. He hadn't come this far to be derided by a bitter old woman. "Poetry and drama. Theatre."

"Ah, I see." Mrs Sharpe tutted and shook her head. "You're a writer."

"I am."

"And what makes you want to do such a foolhardy job?"

"I don't know. You may as well ask me why I have blue eyes."

"Are ye any good?"

"I think I am," replied the young man. "I just need to convince everyone else."

"Convince London and you'll convince the world, is that it?"

"I ask only for a chance. An opportunity," Will replied. "London is where the great theatres are. The great actors. It would be silly not to go."

"Yes, well." Mrs Sharpe sniffed and her boil swelled. "All that glisters ain't gold, sir. That's all I shall say on the matter."

There followed a mellow silence as they watched Bess circle above their heads, in long, slow, graceful gyres.

"I read some of them scraps, mind," Mrs Sharpe said suddenly. "Afore the pigs got 'em. Their desire was greater than mine, see."

"Oh."

She turned to Will and he saw, just for a moment, the very beautiful young girl she must have once been. Yes, there she was, Mary Sharpe – perhaps eight years old, plump and bonny, eyes turning slitty when she laughed, knotty red hair, chuckling without a care in the world. An infectious laugh which had cheered everyone up who'd heard her. He could see her in a bonny hat, dirty from work, jesting and gossiping with whoever was close at hand. "What did you think of what you read, may I ask, Mrs Sharpe?"

"Not bad," sniffed Mrs Sharpe. "Too much punning for my taste. A very low form of wit, is punning. You'll find more than enough of that in the *Benbow* of an evening."

"Ah." Will nodded. "Fair point."

"The Master liked them, I'll say."

"Ah. Did he?" *The Master*, thought Will. *So that's what they call him.*

"He wants ye to stay awhile."

Will bowed. "I'd be happy to."

"Teaching, you'll note. Not writing. You'll do that nonsense in your spare time, like everyone else. During daylight hours you'll put your talent to some practical use. Something that'll make you some money."

"Of course."

"He's too old to teach them himself now, you know. Though he won't stop. He won't stop until he drops dead, which can't be long coming, Gawd help him."

Will looked back at the ruins. "How many pupils are here, ma'am?"

Mrs Sharpe rolled her eyes. "That's a good question." Her mood altered in a blink and she ducked down, squinting. "Hi, she's got something! Look at the way her tail's wagging! Ah, me Bess's got something all right!"

"How can you see that from here?"

"Eyes like a hawk," Mrs Sharpe replied, looking straight at Will. "My father, God Bless His Soul, always said that. Said, you're not a bonny lass, Mare, but ye've got the eyes of a hawk. And he was not far wrong. We're all given something, you see. Key to everything is working out what you've been given. Putting it to good use. Ah! Here she comes. Come on then, my lovely. Come home. Come on then."

As Bess came back to them, wings beating audibly, a dead, wide-eyed hare dangling from her talons, Will watched Mrs Sharpe, smiling and unguarded, and saw the whole story. Her father, he was sure, had died young, perhaps of the plague or the pox. Her mother also, not long after. Mrs Sharpe had brought up the family. She was the oldest child: she was called Mary after all.

Hard work and hard living had ruined her; the old monk had taken her in, perhaps as a housekeeper, perhaps as a schoolmistress, perhaps, even, as a mistress. But probably not, Will thought, seeing it all, reading the woman's elbows and knees.

Probably she'd wanted him to love her but he was too holy, too pious. She'd turned mannish, cold and bitter and her body had become a prison: a fortress wherein that little redheaded, happy plump girl was chained up in a dungeon, deep in the innards. Kept prisoner by her older self.

Poor woman.

Mrs Sharpe was showing Will the dead, still-warm hare and stroking Bess.

"My friend! Good morning to ye! Good morning!"

Will turned. The old monk was standing with the ruins of the monastery behind him, a full moon pale as bone imprinted on the sky above the tower, waving to Will with his great, dark sleeves.

"Come along, then!" he shouted. "Don't you want to start work, boy?"

"Yes, Master," Will replied, nodding to Mrs Sharpe and winking at Bess.

6

"The Magistrate meeting this morning has been cancelled," Alain told Kizzie. He looked around and over her shoulder as he spoke. "I thought you should know. They told me you were here."

"Oh." Kizzie looked back at The Dips. The jewelled ribbons she'd hung in the trees were still there, fluttering and tinkling, but the others were gone. "All right. Thanks for telling me."

"Was that Gillian I saw with you?"

As soon as Alain asked this, Kizzie relaxed. She looked back and said, "Yes. She was here, yes. I don't know where she is now. I thought she was behind me."

"Who else was here?"

"My sister Athy and Zak. He's a boy in our class." She put her hand to her brow, which she would never normally do, but which seemed somehow right. "Where on earth have they gone?"

"What were you all doing down here?"

Kizzie shrugged. "Just clearing our heads before breakfast. Got a nightmare assignment to hand in today. We're a group. Not Athy, but she knows about some of that stuff. Boring stuff."

Alain seemed preoccupied. They began to walk back up by the sixth form block towards the Assembly Hall. A bell rang loudly throughout the school. Pupils were filing into the hall from all directions.

"Did you talk to her about me?" Alain asked.

"I tried," Kizzie explained, shrugging, "but I don't think she took me seriously."

"I'm serious."

"I know you are. It's just that it's not...normal. I don't think she thinks you could really be interested in her, that's all."

This seemed to cheer Alain up. As they got near the main intersection, busy with day students arriving and boarders coming out of breakfast, Alain pulled Kizzie to one side. "I need to tell you something. I mean, you are practically one of us now, so I should tell you."

"What?"

"There is someone here, in the school, who is not what they seem." Alain pushed back his fringe. "It's someone who is not real. An imaginary character."

"What?"

"I know, I know, but you have to believe me. There is something here. An entity. A dangerous entity. Do you remember the boy you saw on the playing fields?"

"Yes." Kizzie looked very confused.

"Well he is not real. Someone invented him."

"Oh-kay."

"I'm telling you because it might save your life." Alain said this in such a serious tone that Kizzie got a fright. "Yes, this information might save the life of your friends – of everyone. There're things going on here that you have no idea about, Kizzie. Creatures like that boy are very dangerous. They're unnatural. They belong somewhere and they're not where they belong." He looked vulnerable. "Please make sure Gillian doesn't go near him. If she does she'll be playing with fire, you must understand that. You must make her understand that. All of you are in great danger if you don't heed my warning. I can't tell you how serious I am."

Kizzie nodded, slightly embarrassed by the scene he was making. "OK, OK, Alain. I get it. We haven't seen him. But – but thanks for telling us anyway. I'll be on the lookout." Kizzie turned to the Assembly Hall and queued to get inside. She had a seat saved for her and walked over.

"What was that all about?" Gillian asked.

"Nothing," said Kizzie.

"Did he see us?" Gillian asked.

"No."

"See who?" asked Angela, drying her wet hair with a small hand towel she'd brought with her.

"No one," replied the other three at the same time.

Alain remained outside the Hall and lifted his nose to the air like a predator.

He knew the boy was out here, somewhere on the grounds. There was no way Alain could go to Assembly that morning. No, he must hunt the boy down.

Not knowing where to start, Alain walked in the opposite direction to the green tide surging towards him, back down the steps and alongside the kitchens to the front drive. There, somewhat pathetically, was one of the boys who'd left the school the year before. He was standing by his car smoking a cigarette, music booming from the speaker in the car door, winking at a sixth-form girl who was backing away from him.

"Can't stay away, huh?" asked Alain, approaching.

"Hey. All that brown-nosing paid off, huh, Vernie? Got your little badge? Free to boss people about now, eh? Official bully."

"You shouldn't be smoking on the school grounds, Doyle."

"Whatcha gonna do? Give me extra homework?"

"What are you doing here, man? You're sad!"

"Just paying a quick trip in to see you losers."

"There's only one loser here, man."

"Yep, you."

Alain gave the other boy a mock salute. "Whatever you say, Doyle."

The Head of the Magistrate walked on down the looping path, beyond Lanark, the senior boy's house, and down to the workmen's sheds. His sixth sense tingled when he walked amongst the tractors and mowers and he spent ten minutes checking under and between the machinery.

He's not here but he was.

Try as he might, Alain couldn't conjure up a picture of who

he'd seen at The Dips with Kizzie. Truth be told he'd been thinking of home: his grandmother was very ill. She had perhaps days, probably hours to live. His mother and father had told him it was better he stayed where he was, concentrated on his studies; it's what his grandmother would have wanted, but the news had thrown Alain. Nobody had died in his family in a long time and he was very close to his grandmother, always had been.

He'd wandered down the side of the sixth form block to be alone and think things through when he'd seen Kizzie approaching. Some other people, figures, had scuttled away into the bushes before he'd had a chance to see who they were. When he'd seen Kizzie he'd thought of Gillian. She was the only thing that balanced out the darkness he felt when he thought of his grandmother.

We'll be good together.

But he had a rival. He knew that.

But he also knew what his rival was. And how to deal with him.

Alain had been at the school long enough to know that the odd characters that showed up from time to time were by and large harmless. They were usually more scared of the school and pupils than anyone could be of them. Most of them came from lost bits of paper, notes or messages written by unsuspecting or sporadic Writers, people the Magistrate hadn't identified and vetted.

The lonely characters were wishes and dreams put down on paper. Sometimes something truly frightening roamed the school but the Master and the Cleaners were usually fast to mop up the bad ones. It was strange that they hadn't this time. Alain was slightly unsure if all this was not really some sort of game on the part of the Master. No fictional creature come to life had ever lasted this long.

This one – *my prey, my rival* – is a worthy match, Alain thought. He was looking forward to the chance of proving himself. Of finishing the contest. *So, where are you?*

Now he was coming up the path behind St Nicholas House and he saw the dried-up puddle where the Master had enlightened him. He afforded himself a smile. *Best not tell that story to anyone who hasn't been through something similar,* he thought. *They might think I'm crazy.*

And then, in the undergrowth by the low stone wall, Alain spotted him: The boy from the fields, crouching down and staring back at Alain from between the spray of shiny, evergreen leaves.

"That's enough!" Alain shouted, and as he did so Romeo bolted from the cover and sprinted down the main path. Alain shot after him and they both ran at top speed, elbows pumping, knees high, around the Main Building. Romeo was going for the playing fields and tried to cut across the back lawn between the school swimming pool and the Assembly Hall but Alain got him halfway, near the fishpond, and rugby tackled him to the floor.

Someone in the Assembly Hall saw the fight, shouted, and within a minute the entire school was pressed against the many windows watching the two boys roll about together on the back lawn. Green uniforms and teachers came streaming out of the glass atrium at the back of the Assembly Hall, but seeing who was involved they formed a line, a kind of barricade, watching and waiting.

"Just stop fighting us and we'll help you," Alain tried, teeth gritted, choking as the other boy's elbow dug into his windpipe. "We can take you back but you must let us help you!"

"Never!" Romeo managed to get his knee and then his foot under Alain's chest and thrust him off with a fierce kick.

As Alain flew backwards, Romeo set off, away from the crowds, up the small incline towards the white fencing surrounding the swimming pool. The pool was covered with a dirty blue tarpaulin for winter, and tied down, and Romeo skipped over the knots making for the other side. Alain, catching fast, vaulted the fence and elected against trying to run across the tarpaulin: he had no choice but to follow the other boy around the edge of the pool.

On the far side, beyond the fence, was the sanctuary of woodland and an alternative route to the playing fields and Romeo might have made it if he hadn't tripped. But he had and he had heavily.

Alain was on him in a second and pinned him down, blood oozing from Romeo's wounds. The Head of the Magistrate sat on the other boy's back and screamed for help and the lines in front of the Assembly Hall broke and teachers and pupils began to flood across the back lawn, around the pond and across to the swimming pool.

Seizing his moment, Romeo spun himself over, tossing Alain onto the tarpaulin, which ripped and gave. There was a splash and a gasp from the boy in the water – it was thick like soup – and, as he struggled for a grip, more and more of the blue tarpaulin gave and tore in Alain's grasping hands.

Romeo didn't stay to watch but forced himself over the low fence, leaving red smudges on the peeling wood, and hobbled away into the greenery like a wounded bird.

When the first teachers and pupils arrived they stopped at the edge of the pool and gasped in horror at the sight of Alain Verne floating just under the murky, dark water, eyes wide open in horror, very pale.

By strange co-incidence, his grandmother died at that exact moment.

7

"This way Mr Shakes-staff."

"That's Shake*speare*, Master."

"Shakespeare, that's right. Watch your step now. Mrs Sharpe made this little bridge and there's many a time I almost slipped off it. The key is balance. Get your bearings before you even step onto it, see?"

"Or perhaps just hop across, Master?"

"Ah, my hopping days are long gone, my young friend." The old monk used Will's shoulder as a guide as he walked the swaying planks. Through the slits lay a shallow, grassy gorge, which might have held a brook or a trickle of water in its deepest crevice. It smelled of human insides and was home to a thousand flies and maggots. When he was sure the Master was across, Will hopped the last of the way and almost toppled back into the filth, catching a sapling just in time to save himself.

"Health is not always a virtue," commented the monk, amused.

They approached the ruins of the old monastery arm in arm, the Master shuffling along like a sleepwalker. Will could hardly walk straight himself, his feet bruised and calloused. Skull-eye windows peered out from the grey stone walls and Will now noticed the smoke puffing its way up into the sky from somewhere behind the high curtain wall, jagged and broken.

"Is this where classes are conducted, Master?"

"In a manner of speaking." The old man prodded the ground with his stick. There were boulders and some masonry scattered about and snaking trails had been cut through the debris, worn to bare earth by human footfalls. The widest of the trails reached a low doorway in the wall which, when ducked through, led to a mossy, dank, cell-like room that reeked to high heaven. "The local badgers sneak in here on the coldest nights," the monk explained, quite out of breath. "And who can blame them?"

Will, intrigued, followed the hunched-over figure as they walked on the squishy, smelly, springy floor into what seemed like pitch darkness. Over the worst of the stench, which came and went, Will could detect the autumnal smell of wood burning in the open air and then a breeze on his fingers and against the tip of his nose.

"If I could only locate the lock," the old monk muttered to himself before a screeching of steel on steel sounded. "My apologies, young man, but that's the gate open. Watch your breeches on the sharp ends and close it after you. Up we go."

Will did as he was told and noticed a leaky light above them. The ground was now quite solid and so cold he could feel it though the thin, patched up soles of his boots.

They were at the bottom of a staircase which wound tightly upwards. The monk went first, slowly, sandals slapping, and Will followed him, marvelling at the marble aspect of the monk's battered, bare feet. The old man's toes were almost purple and the nails so misshapen and yellow they were like claws. Whatever was he doing almost barefoot in this weather anyway?

"Come along come along, squeeze past me," the Master wheezed at the top, pressing himself against the brick wall as Will went on to emerge in the corner of an open courtyard. Only, it wasn't a courtyard, it was obviously the chapel of the old church. There were graves on the floor and tombs in the remaining walls. Sackcloth, straining and sagging, was hanging half-heartedly across the space but open sky shone down on the altar and remains of the chancel. "Now where the devil is everyone?" asked the monk.

As if in reply three figures emerged from the shadows on the other side of the space, a woman and two men, and the monk nodded happily.

"There you are, there you are! My dears, this is Mr Shackspere. The one I was telling you about."

"Shakespeare," corrected Will.

The tallest of the young men – both were no older than twenty – stepped forwards and smiled warmly. He was tall, athletic, well-dressed and very well-mannered. "Good morning to you, Mr Shakespeare. Very nice to have you here with us."

"Very nice to be here," Will replied, thinking, *Are these the pupils or the masters?* He turned to the other man – smaller, darker, arms-folded and scowling from over his ruffled collar – and nodded. The only woman was standing slightly behind this angry figure, perhaps smiling. She was dark-skinned, surely African, Will thought, and quite marvellously, windingly beautiful. He felt his gaze stick to her and his eyes refused to blink.

The lady was so stunning to behold Will had to make a conscious effort to remove his cap, bowing low and feeling a terrible shame when he looked at the mess of material he wore on his head dangling from his dirty hand like a filleted ferret. He knew how important first impressions were: what must she have thought of him?

"Good day to you, sir," the lady whispered, in a voice so low it was hard for Will to catch anything of her personality in her voice.

Will straightened in time to see the angry man-in-black step forward to address the monk. "Correct me if I'm wrong, Master, but you said it would be only the three of us here."

"It was only you," nodded the monk, hands in his sleeves, "and now it is again. Only you. Four."

"The library is almost finished, my Master," said the first boy, the tall, elegant one, who put out his hand towards a door in the shadows. "Perhaps you would like to see it?"

The Master nodded. "Yes, I think we all would."

As they walked across the open space together there were handshakes. The tall, amiable boy was Ayland; the shorter, fiery one Uric. The lady was Bethsabe and smelled, to Will, who walked in her wake, as exotic as she looked. The monk, whom they all called Master, Will noted, led them into the dingy buildings again but this time there were fires lit at intervals and torches on the walls and apart from one awful corridor, no vile smells to make Will retch.

They crossed another small courtyard, the sky like a glaring, white roof, and descended another set of stairs into darkness. At the foot of these stairs the Master opened a wooden door, which creaked impressively, and they all stepped into a great chamber, curved like a cellar, lit by myriad candles and two candelabras, filled along every wall and in stacks like pillars, by books. Hundreds and hundreds of books.

"Ah! Wonderful!" cried the Master, clasping his hands together. "This has made me so happy! God Bless You All!"

"Which means we can begin our real work now, does it?" tried Uric, who spoke every utterance with a look of pain.

"But you have been working!" The Master was walking with Bethsabe in and out of the pillars of words and leather. "What else have you been doing, Uric, my child? What do you call all this?"

Will couldn't help but wander in wonder along the arrays, reading the names on the spines, stopping, sometimes, to ponder a title he found interesting. *Oh what I could do with all this knowledge*, he thought. And he was ashamed that the first thing he could think of doing was stealing a book or two and making a run for it.

Will's weakness was history and here he was in a room made out of history books. Why, with just one of these tomes he could write fifteen plays! He was an alchemist when it came to words – hadn't they all said that back at home? Hadn't he always said that? *Give me the raw materials and I will give you gold!*

"Mr Shaxper! Oh, Mr Shaxper! Do join us! I have something to say."

"Shakespeare," said Will as he came to rejoin the group.

The Master was holding a large book in his hands. It looked like a ledger, the type Will had seen many times in his father's office.

"This is The Book of the School," the Master told them all. His eyes were completely blue; a weird, crystal blue which was opaque yet milky. "Now that you have prepared Its home, The Book has come to live among you. Only one of you may ever write in it."

"Who?" asked Uric.

"You," replied the Master, to Uric. Will felt a sting of jealousy before the Master added, "Or perhaps you, or you," and he went on around them all.

Uric was nodding, trying to smile, but he smiled like a shark. "How will we know, Master? When we should write in The Book?"

But the Master was already moving away from them. He had left The Book on top of a narrow stack. All of them felt it wasn't proper to say anything until the old man was out of their presence. They watched him until he left.

"He's always so desperate to conjure up an air of mystery," Uric complained, turning and lancing an invisible opponent with a thrust of his sword.

"He's deaf as a post," Bethsabe replied, smiling, and Will was stunned by the effect. It was like a sunlight on glass. "He simply didn't hear what you said."

"Well, hello again, Will," Ayland said, shaking Will's hand again and raising an eyebrow. "You've come here just as we did, without too much of an idea of the whys and wherefores of what this is all about. But despite some of us being rather impatient, we do seem to be getting somewhere. Slowly. Things do begin to make sense if you go with, rather than against, the flow."

"May we take any of these books?" Will asked. "To read, I mean? While we're here?"

"Yes, yes."

"That's your pay," grunted Uric, who was crouching down and reading book spines near the foot of a pile.

"Would you like to see your room?" Ayland asked Will.

"Ah!" Bethsabe wagged a finger at Ayland. "What a clever chap you are! You said the spare quarters would be for another of us!"

"What I want to know," called out Uric, his voice echoing off the curved brickwork above them, "is when are the damned pupils going to arrive?"

"Oh, Uric," replied Ayland, motioning for Will to follow him. "Can't you see that they already have?"

Wednesday

1

"This is it," Kizzie whispered, sliding the large, rectangular, ledger-like book off the shelf. She put on a fake, portentous voice. "The Book! *Da-da-daaah!*"

"Are you actually allowed to touch it?" Zak was more amused than afraid.

"Why not?"

They were in the Eleusinian Room during the lull between the end of lessons and the start of afternoon activities. Meek, lime-yellow light bled in from the stained-glass window in the high turret tower below which four storeys of caged books were visible through the steel scaffolding. All the access ladders were locked up and fastened in place.

Zak and Kizzie, standing together on a leather-seated chair, stared at The Book. The limp school flag hung off the panelled wall in front of them like an unwatered plant above a mantelpiece dotted with matches, candles and other paraphernalia used in the Magistrate ceremonies which took place here. Both of them knew that despite everything else in the room, The Book was the big prize. The Book was the school's number one treasure.

"How come you can even get in here without permission?" Despite his bravado, Zak's eyes flickered to the main door. "Isn't this, like, top secret?"

"I'm a library volunteer and a House Consul," Kizzie explained breezily. "They trust me." She kissed his cheek. "When I'm promoted, this place'll be like my second home."

"You're not supposed to touch this though, surely?"

"Well, really, nobody can do anything with this book unless they're a Writer and right now Sam – the Head Boy – is the only one. He obviously decided it's OK." Kizzie shrugged. "If it's survived five hundred years or whatever it is, I'm sure it can survive today. Anyway, they use it for ceremonies and stuff, you've seen it on School Day —"

"No. Don't think so."

"Course you have. It doesn't matter anyway, it's not like it's going to explode or anything if you touch it. I've had a look loads of times, loads of us have. It's just a book. It's only got power if you believe in it, you know, like the Wizard of Oz. It's just paper and leather and rules and stuff. Who cares about all that, anyway – I just think it's cool, reading some of the stuff inside. Some of it's so old!"

"The bit I don't get is what you were telling me before." Zak stroked his chin. Kizzie had opened The Book and they were reading a paragraph of copperplate, cursive writing on the first page; some kind of dedication. "If you're a Writer, what does that mean?"

"It means – supposedly – that anything you write in this book comes to pass."

"What?"

"Seriously. That's what they believe."

"But it's all rubbish, right?" Zak shook his head. "Honestly. People believe the craziest stuff."

"I know," said Kizzie. "Nutters." But as she caught Zak's eye, a thought crossed her mind that she never wanted to think again. She blocked it out immediately. "Superstitious crap."

"That's just it though, isn't it?" Zak stepped down off the chair. He had to walk on tiptoes to avoid his cowboy boots clip-clopping too noisily on the parquet floor. "It's like the people who say they can sense when someone is going to message them. They look at their phone and – hey! – there's a message, or a message arrives at the same time. But they forget the ten million times they look at their phone and there's no message. It's just people looking for meaning in a meaningless world!"

"Why do you wear cowboy boots?" Kizzie had set The Book back in its place and joined Zak on the floor.

"I always wanted to be a cowboy. An outlaw."

"Really?"

Zak nodded. "Yep. It's been my ambition for as long as I can remember. You know how other people want to be pilots or policemen or lawyers? I want to be a cowboy."

Kizzie thought about this and said, "I've always wanted to be a rainbow."

"Each to their own."

"Or a sunset."

"Now you know what to write in that book if you ever have the power."

"Ha," replied Kizzie.

Zak put a finger to his lip. "You know something weird? I don't remember when I came here. To the school, I mean." His face was very open. "I just heard myself saying that I've always wanted to be a cowboy and I don't really know if I'm just saying that, making it up, I mean, or if it's true. I can't even remember buying these boots!"

"Lay off the drugs, maaan." Kizzie was now nose to nose with him and she crouched slightly so that she was looking up into his eyes. "There are more important things to think about," Kizzie whispered to him. "Like us."

"I seriously can't remember anything about my childhood." Zak shook his head. "Don't you think that's weird? Maybe I've blocked it out but I can't remember anything. I mean, nothing. Zilch."

"I think you're lucky. You live in the present. That's a talent not many people have."

"I'm serious."

"I'm Kizzie."

"You're impossible."

"Kiss me."

"Ah ha! So that's why you brought me here!"

"Oh, just kiss me, Zak! I can't wait anymore!"

So he did.

2

The Master appeared to each person in the room in a different form. The curtains were drawn and the only light was that flickering from embers in the grate.

To Mr Firmin, the Headmaster, The Master was a swirling, floating wave of dark ocean hovering in the centre of the office.

To Alain Verne, he was a smiling young man with a beatific aspect. Alain, watching, was stony-faced, determined to exact revenge for coming so close to death.

To Sam Cauldhame, the Master was the Headmaster as a skeleton wearing shreds of flesh-like torn clothes. He was a skeleton Sam had seen years before on an archaeological dig with his father: a sight that had given him nightmares for years. It was very like the Master to know this and appear in such a guise.

For Leana, the Master was an old crone, hideously disfigured, one of the many witches she'd seen as a girl and who'd brought her up. She too was unmoved. The seriousness of the Master's manifestation underlined the seriousness of the problem they were gathered there to try to resolve.

To me, the writer, the Master is an empty cowl which stares out of this white page behind the black swirls of the letters and whispers words in my ear.

To you, the reader, search your imagination for the form he takes. Take a moment to connect with him in your mind's eye.

The atmosphere in the office was very sombre.

The horrible attempt on Alain's life was fresh in everyone's minds. Things had almost taken a deadly turn and there was little doubt that the situation must be rectified at once.

"You're quite sure he's still here somewhere?" Mr Firmin asked.

"He cannot escape," the Master replied.

"Then we catch him and banish him," Sam answered, "however we can."

"Why can't we find him?" Firmin asked, banging his fist down on the desk. "We've managed to save Alain and we've controlled worse crises than this before. Why can't we find the bugger and send him away?"

"He is protected by the Writer," the Master replied. "By the Writer's story. There are consequences. There will be consequences."

"That's what we have to find out," Sam declared. "Who wrote this story? Who is behind all of this? Who created him?"

"It has to be a member of the Magistrate," Leana said. "Someone with a grudge against Alain."

"What I can't understand," Mr Firmin began, coming around the desk to where they all were, "is that there's no sign of the story in The Book. No sign of anything. I mean, is it possible there are two Books?"

"The pages were regenerated," was The Master's answer.

"Regenerated," echoed Leana.

"Someone tore out a page?" Sam realised, stunned.

"This is someone who knows what they're doing," Mr Firmin said.

"Or not," came The Master.

Each stared at their vision.

"The Writer is a living person," the Master told them. "They are one of your own. They are not cruel, cunning or wise. Quite the opposite. They are opportunistic, lucky and green. They don't know what they're doing. They have no idea about the sanctity of human life. They're playing a game and they're all the more dangerous for doing so."

"But who is it?" asked Leana.

The Master conjured up the guilty figure as a hollow-eyed face in the flames.

"Really?" gasped Leana.

"But how?" Sam asked, gobsmacked.

Leana had one hand on the door handle, ready to leave. "I'll go now!"

"No!" The Master's voice was solid. "First, banish the Infiltrator."

"But how?" asked Sam. "You said he can't be caught!"

"I think I see where the Master is going with this," said Mr Firmin, calm suddenly. "One step at a time."

"The story is written," the Master added, before vanishing.

"Sam," Mr Firmin said, pointing. "Open The Book. No time to lose."

"I'm going for the culprit," Leana announced, leaving.

"The Master told me there was no way for the boy to escape," Alain Verne said, sitting forwards on his chair. "He told me that when he came to see me. You're wasting your time."

"You also said he told you to beware of water," Sam replied, checking his pen was working by tapping the nib on the back of his hand. A blue dot formed.

Alain nodded. "I'm part of the story," he said, simultaneously realising the truth of what he was saying.

"We all are," Firmin told him, slightly impatiently. "And it's not our place to know how it ends, you know that, so start concentrating on how we're going to resolve this."

"What do you want me to write, sir?" asked Sam, kneeling over The Book. Until this episode had begun, he'd thought he was the only Writer at the school.

"Let's see," Mr Firmin said, stroking his chin before beginning to speak.

Outside, in the corridor, Leana was concentrating so hard on what she had to do that she didn't notice the girl with bad skin running towards her. They collided and Leana threw up her hands. "Watch it!"

"Please, miss – er, I mean, Leana."

"I'm busy."

"No, it's just..."

"I'm busy, I said!" She strode off down the lime-green carpet, turning to add, "Honestly, if you knew the importance of the task in hand, you'd wouldn't even think of interrupting me!"

"But I keep thinking I see William Shakespeare!" Angela whispered, watching the head girl go.

3

Gillian looked out at the full moon, which was furry at the edges although the sky was cloudless. "I think the sky is really changing colour this time, you know."

"Impossible. Your eyes are getting used to the light."

"No, really. I think it's morning. You should go."

Romeo sat up. "I'm not going. They can come and get me here."

"Oh, why is this happening to us? That's what I don't get. Why can't it just be easy? The usual way? Why does it have to be like this?"

"I don't care if they come and get me. What are they going to do? What could they do to me?"

Gillian pulled him closer. Behind her, on the faded white wall, now grey, was a years-old cartoon of a child being given an injection. "No one's going to take you away from me."

"I love you, you know." He was facing her, eye to eye, soul to soul. "No, I really do. I know people say it all the time. I know I've said it before and not meant it, but this time I mean it. This is something I've never felt before. It's so simple and clear."

"It's the truth," said Gillian quietly.

"Exactly. It's the truth. It's quiet as the truth. The truth is always quiet, isn't it?"

"We'll always be together."

"I love you so much."

"I love you!"

"Why didn't I just tell you back then, when we met? In the bar at home?"

"Ha, why didn't you?"

"I don't know." Romeo was asking himself the same question but suddenly saw he was many people, not one. He was no longer who he had been. He was only this: with her now, in love. To be here he had to have been there. He had to have done nothing. "I was a fool."

"My fool," said Gillian. "And I'm a fool, too, you know. I didn't do anything, either, did I?"

"I didn't trust myself. Maybe I thought you were going to laugh at me. Or, or…"

"You know I think that even if you'd said something I wouldn't have believed you." Gillian stared out at the sky. "Oh, no, it really is changing colour. I'm serious!"

"Don't look at it."

There was a sudden noise, a bump, from somewhere outside the Sick Bay door. It had come from one of the dorms alongside or upstairs. Both shifted in the narrow bed; the world had changed. It was no longer theirs.

"I have to go," Romeo said.

"Tell me we'll see each other again."

"I promise."

Gillian suddenly drew back and scrunched herself up against the headboard as he stood in front of the window. "Oh, I don't know if it's the light or what but you look terrible. You look like a corpse."

Romeo wanted to joke but instead, the truth working through him, he shook his head, swallowed and whispered, "You too. You look like a statue on a tomb."

Both turned at a knock and they said goodbye with their eyes as the door began to open. In the time it took the Matron to come in, Romeo fled.

"What are you doing with this bally window open?" the Matron asked, clipping it closed and shuffling back to the bed in her slippers. "No wonder the windows are rattling. You've created a right good draught." She put the back of her left palm against Gillian's head. "You're cold, lovey. That's not good. Not good at all. Means your fever's rising."

Gillian lay back on the pillows as Matron shuffled away down the creaking corridor.

She saw his shadow through the curtains, in the dark window and crawled out of bed and hopped over the floor, but if he'd been there, he was gone.

Only the moon, furred at the edges, fading into the day.

And the sad, sad echo of fading happiness in her heart.

Thursday

1

Bethsabe sat in front of the empty stone hole of a window and watched the snow falling. All was quiet. The room was deathly cold and Bethsabe had a shawl pulled up over her shoulders. She turned as she heard Will coming in through the open doorway.

"Ah, hello," he said, obviously surprised, sniffing through his swollen, red nose. He was carrying two great volumes of history which he set down on his wooden table, the only furniture in the low, cold room besides the bed. "You didn't light the fire."

"I don't know how and it's too cold," Bethsabe replied. She turned back to the silent, white storm. "I don't think I ever want to stop finding snow magical."

"There's been plenty this winter." Will knelt and started the fire. He rubbed his hands happily over the crackling kindling and slapped his sides as he stood up. "Would you like a tea? Something to eat?"

"No, I'm sorry. I came to ask you a question and I saw the…" She fluttered a pretty, patterned sleeve at the view and shook her head. "I find it quite hypnotic. Still."

As I do you, Will might have said. It had been a shock to find Bethsabe here, he'd hardly spoken to her since their first meeting. If one of them wasn't in class or working in the underground library, she was usually guarded by Uric, who, Will guessed, was her husband or boyfriend. "And to what do I owe the pleasure of this visit?"

"I like your play about the young lovers," Bethsabe said. She looked at Will with her dark eyes. Her long lashes flickered slowly open and closed, very much on purpose.

"Ah! Been reading my personal papers, have you?" Will turned his back, blew on his hands and began to arrange the cups and kettle, silently thrilled.

"They were right there on the shelf. I put my hand on them as

I came in. A page fell off. I read it. The rest is history."

"But why did you come in here?"

"I was looking for you." Bethsabe stood. She was tall and had to stoop to avoid touching the cobwebs on the rafters with her hair. When she opened her shawl to adjust her position, Will thought she looked like some magical creature which had been conjured up by the Winter gods. "I wanted to talk to you, Will."

"Really," stuttered the young man in response, settling the black kettle on a tripod over the flames with a clatter. "What about?"

"I don't know. Just talk."

"Does Uric know you're here?"

"No."

Bethsabe took a step closer, but Will backed off. He picked up a sheaf of paper from the shelf. "How much did you read? I've made revisions. It's not finished yet."

"Enough. It's very beautiful. Very dramatic!" She sat again near the fire and smiled at him. "How do you come up with such things?"

"I steal them," Will replied, tapping the two history books he'd brought in.

Bethsabe laughed. "What's the matter, Will? Are you scared of me?"

"A little bit," Will replied. The kettle was beginning to smoke. He stood with both hands curled behind his back, leaning on the blue stone wall. "I'm a married man, Bethsabe."

"Oh." She nodded. "I see."

"I have two young children. I'm trying to make my way in the world to make a better life for them." He turned serious. It hurt him having to say all this. He'd liked it better when they'd admired each other from afar, when it had all been unreal. Now it was real and ugly. "I appreciate your comments on my work, though. I only wish a few playhouse owners agreed with you."

"Don't you believe your plays are good?" There was a slight

aloofness about her now. She was wounded, covering up.

"Ha! What does that matter?" The kettle began to whistle and Will went over to it. He spooned in sugar, lifted the kettle off the heat and set it down on a slate tray on the table. He felt ridiculous. One part of him wanted to turn to her, fall to her knees and proclaim his love but he couldn't. Now he must play the victor, the rejecter, and he hated hurting her.

"If you don't believe in your own stories, who will?"

"Fine sentiments," nodded Will. "Very true. I must remember that."

"Where I come from belief is everything, Will. The whole world is magical. Existence is magical."

"Well, I come from Stratford," Will began, "and in Stratford things are rather more..." But his voice trailed off as he saw Bethsabe had vanished. Gone completely.

Will ran across to the window and looked out but he could only see virgin snow and the hard, black edges of some fallen stones.

The whiteness was thick and compact.

He glanced up at the rafters – grey, dusty balls of webbing – and peered under the table before rushing back to the door. Still there was nothing, only snow. Snow in the sky, snow on the ground. On the shelf by the door he saw his much-blotched script piled in order. The seat where she had been sitting a few moments earlier was icy cold to the touch.

My mind is playing tricks on me.

I am in love with her.

Bethsabe! My dark lady!

I am obsessed with you and now I am imagining you in my life.

In my room!

He ducked outside into the snow, into the cold, and his half-thawed ears throbbed.

It was his troubled conscience which had been speaking, talking out loud about his wife, his children, unseen but there, of course, always there.

How can you love her when you don't even know her?

Think of Anne. Think of Hamnet. Think of home, of what you have!

A few minutes later, with a shock, Will looked up and realised he didn't know where he was. He turned and saw, or thought he saw, buildings or trees or sky, but really he saw nothing, only falling snow; snow falling everywhere, as though the white sky was breaking, flaking apart.

And then he felt someone collide with him, a young maid he recognised – girl from the school perhaps, one of the stable-hands or one of Mrs Sharpe's helpers in the kitchen.

"I beg your pardon."

The maid who had fallen dragged back her hair. *"Who are you?"*

"I want the school," Will said, not knowing what to say. Speaking aloud, he noticed how cold he was. His lips were numb.

"Which school?" the maid asked, circling him as though he were an apparition.

How must I look? Will thought. *Like a ghost – see the way she stares at me!* "The school. The school I know is hereabouts."

"Who are you?"

"I might ask you the same question, ma'am."

"Madam?"

"If you would be so kind as to show me the way to the school, I would be much obliged." But the girl backed away into the snow on all fours, stomach up, face screwed up in confusion and fear, and she began to disappear. "Don't go!" Will cried, following after her, losing her, but trudging on, trusting, somewhere, that he was going in the right direction.

He could hear Bethsabe's voice in his mind – *it's your voice! You're making all this up!* – saying, "I believe in magic. The whole world is magical" and his eyelashes began to freeze over. And he began to feel sleepy.

And he may have walked for hours or seconds.

Until he saw something, someone, in the snow ahead of him.

A dead body.

A grey body.

A boy sitting in the snow, naked, head bowed.

Despite the cold, Will tore off his jacket and threw it around the boy's bare shoulders. Looking up, praying for help, he caught sight of the warm, bright glow of the school building and cried, "Yes, God!" with relief.

2

Gillian hadn't slept and she was feeling reckless.

She didn't really care what she did or said. The only thing she wanted was to be with him again but she knew he'd gone. She knew he'd been taken away. Perhaps somewhere inside herself she wanted to keep control of her emotions and not let anyone know what she was feeling, but the whole world seemed like a great joke, some kind of torture. Life really was not worth living without him.

She ate breakfast mechanically. Got her books. Walked up to The Quad without knowing what the weather was like. She was numb outside and in. During English she sat next to Angela who prodded her and told her stories about the strange man she'd seen again when she was out running. "I swear it's this bloke," Angela had said, tapping the black and white portrait at the front of the play they were reading. "Shakeswhatever."

"So?"

"Oh, very nice."

Ah, the torture of English. *Romeo and Juliet*, of course. Gillian had hummed, counted and stared at the cracks in the walls, anything not to have to concentrate on the words and names: his name. Why was life like this? When you didn't want to see or hear anything about something it was all around you. Sometimes everything moved so slowly it seemed as though nothing was going to happen, but other times it all changed and moved so quickly, almost too quickly.

The sea, she thought. *I am like an ocean, always changing, always the same. I am an Ocean planet, pulled this way and that by forces beyond my control. When I fly too near the sun I boil under clouds like Venus. I erupt. As I float away from the nearest star I freeze over, but there is life in my depths. Fossils. Reminders that there was once life here.*

These thoughts calmed her.

Gillian pictured herself adrift on a vast ocean, somewhere in the middle of nowhere with nothing to see but water and sky. It was late afternoon and the sea was a deep, milky blue and there she was in the middle of it, a drop but also part of the whole. It was warm there, bobbing on the waves, sinking in the troughs. Perhaps she had fallen from the sky, or off the back of the boat. She had no fear of the sea creatures and no fear of death. She was part of the world, all right for the moment, bobbing like a cork or a dinghy.

She would lie on her back and look up at the sky. The clouds looked like breaking waves might from the seabed. She thought about the wonder of the earth: of the atmosphere, of weather, of oxygen and life. She was lying in liquid, which only managed to stay stuck to the rock because of the speed at which the rock was turning. The rock was small, in the scheme of things, one of many rocks swirling around a giant ball of fire, but that ball of fire was also rather small. There were many balls of fire, most bigger than hers, swirling around a dark centre like water going down a plughole. And there were many of these starry whirlpools spinning at different points in the vast universe, itself expanding into nothing, creating itself, starting and ending.

The universe didn't care if she lived or died but *he* did, wherever he was, and she could still feel the burn of his kiss on her lips, the thrill of his touch in the palms of her hands and the searing brand of her love burnt into her heart.

She could see him and feel him but she knew he wasn't there – *here* – and, snapping her eyes open and walking out of the class as though hypnotised, she knew she had to find him.

She would do anything to find him and be with him. Nothing else was important: nothing else in the world.

We must only be together.

If he has gone, I will go where he has gone.

"Gillian?"

Gil looked up and saw Kizzie in the reflection in the window. In another mood, on another day, she might have noticed that Kizzie was not her usual self. She might have noticed she looked drawn and sad. But Gillian, after a quick nod of the head, continued folding clothes.

"What are you doing?"

"Packing."

"For what?"

Gillian looked up to think of an answer but she couldn't really put into words what she wanted to say. "I don't know. To see him. I'm going, that's all I know."

"But where?" Kizzie closed the dorm door and came around to lean against the desk in front of the window, right in front of Gillian.

"I don't know. Don't try and stop me, Kiz, I'm not in the mood."

"How can you find him if you don't know where he is?"

I'll follow my heart, Gillian wanted to say. That made sense in her head but there was no way she could say it out loud. "I'm just gonna look."

"You don't think he's in the school?"

"No."

"How do you know?"

Gillian looked at Kizzie properly for the first time. There was something about her which was different. "I don't know. A feeling. Why?"

"Because you're right," Kizzie answered. Kizzie couldn't look Gillian in the eye. Kizzie had taken off one of her special rings and was tracing a shape in the dust on the desk. Without thinking she had made a heart.

"How do you know?"

Kizzie blew out a long lungful of air. "Oh, Gil. I'm sorry. I'm so, so sorry."

"Kiz? What's going on?"

"I've done something."

Gillian straightened up. "What?"

"I made him come here."

Gillian took a moment to process the information. "You? How?"

"I wrote it all down."

Gillian cocked her head. "You made him come here? Romeo?"

Kizzie nodded. "Yep."

"Kizzie, what the hell's going on?"

Kizzie backed away to her bed and sat down. She talked as she looked down at her hands. "I made him come here. You told me the story about him, about meeting him on holiday. I wanted to make you happy. You know I have Library activity. They let me in the Eleusinian Room. Well –" she smiled at Gillian sadly and shrugged – "looks like I have The Power." Then, quietly, "Or. I did."

"Where is he now?"

"I don't know."

"Kizzie?"

"I don't know. I thought he was here." She looked at the door. "Maybe they've written him away, I don't know. I only know they found out. Firmin and the Magistrate. Sam and Leana. They've changed things. Sam wrote it. Somehow they found out. I didn't think they would."

"Kizzie what were you thinking?"

"I didn't do it to hurt anyone! I didn't think it would work!"

"But they told you they wanted to promote you, didn't they?"

"I wrote it way before all of that. Ages ago. One day. One stupid day, and I don't even know why. It was stupid. I'm stupid!"

"Incredible."

"At least you met him," Kizzie tried, quietly.

Gillian stared at her in silence. "I'm going."

"Wait, Gil."

"I'm done with you. Stay out of my life!"

"But there's something. I've been thinking. There's something we can do."

Gillian stopped, folded her arms and stared again at the other girl. "What?"

"Alain."

"What?"

"Alain Verne."

"He's dead."

"He survived. I've seen him this morning."

Gillian was about to remonstrate when she thought, *get to the crux of this.* "What about him?"

"He can help us. You." Kizzie stood up. "He can help him, too – Romeo."

"What? Kizzie? What are you thinking? No more riddles!"

"Look, I'm in trouble, all right? I know that. They've spoken to me – whatever power I had – which I didn't even know I had, all right? – has gone. They've taken that away from me. I have School Service until I die, basically, and can't go home until, like, next Christmas, but that's fine. That's like – whatever. I deserve it, or whatever. Maybe. I don't know. But what hurts it me is what you're feeling. I never wanted this, Gil. I just wanted to make you happy, you know. We were studying *Romeo and Juliet*, you were talking about that guy, I had just got together with Zak, everything was great. I just wanted everything to be great for you too. I didn't want any of this."

"But what's this all got to do with Alain Verne?"

Another long sigh came from Kizzie. "He said he'll help you."

Gillian re-crossed her arms. "Help me how?"

"Help you know what happened to Romeo. Make sure he's all right. Maybe even get a message to him."

"Why?"

"Because he likes you, Gil. He feels sorry for you, you know.

Plus, he can. I can't now, so he's the only one who can do it."

Gillian thought about this. "You spoke to him?"

"Just now. I had to. They made me go there and apologise for nearly killing him."

"I don't get why he wants to help me?"

"I told you. Because he likes you. He doesn't want to see you sad."

"And that's it? He's going to do it just to be nice?"

"Yes!" Kizzie folded back the duvet and straightened her pillowcase. "And, like, he said, you know, that maybe you would think about going out with him?"

"*What*?"

"No – Gillian, no! Come back." Kizzie got between the other girl and the door. "Stop!"

"Let me out!"

"He didn't say you *had to* go out with him, just that you'd think about it."

"Move, Kizzie!"

"Gillian, he likes you!" Kizzie searched out Gillian's eyes. "Think about it. This could work for you. This is the most sensible thing!"

"It's disgusting!"

"You never want to see him again, then – your husband – is that it?"

Gillian stood back. "What?"

"Because that's what's going to happen if you pass this up."

"I can't."

"Just think about it." Kizzie took her chance and led Gillian by the shoulders towards her own bed. "Sit down. Let's just talk about this calmly."

"This is terrible."

"This is a chance, though. Your best chance."

"Has he really gone?"

Kizzie knew she meant Romeo. "He has."

"Where?"

"They didn't say. Perhaps back to the island? Italy? Home? I don't know."

Gillian brightened. "I could go there!"

"They said they'd banished him." Kizzie sighed. "Something tells me he's not going to be that easy to find."

"Where did you bring him from?"

"I don't know. I only mentioned that he looked like the boy from the island. I don't know if he was the real boy or someone else. I have no idea. I just wrote what I wrote. I wasn't thinking. It was a bit of fun." Her voice trailed off at the end of the sentence.

"And Alain?" Gillian choked a little on the name. "Can he help me find him?"

"He said he'd help you know if he was all right," Kizzie explained. "That's as far as he would go when I talked to him. But you can talk to him. You can ask him to do what you want."

"But I have to be – what? – his girlfriend?"

Kizzie nodded quickly and half-closed her eyes. She was up on tiptoes. "More or less."

Gillian buried her head in her hands and groaned.

"When you find out Romeo's all right, you can dump him, I guess," Kizzie said, resting a consoling hand on Gillian's shoulder.

3

Will Shakespeare was sitting alone on the back lawn beside the frozen fishpond.

He was thinking about the images which had come to him in the night, images he didn't know what to do with.

Sometimes whole stories came to him, visions, which he could see and hear but couldn't remember long enough to write down. That night the images had driven him from the warmth of his bed, outside to look at the few stars he could see in the sky. He felt unslept and dislocated, as though he might be hovering just above his own head, looking down at his growing bald spot – *ah! Still too young for this!* – and the black eye of the fishpond next to his hat.

Little things please little minds, he thought, remembering Ovid, which he'd been browsing before bed. Ah, he'd always had these problems, ever since he was a child. He'd never slept well. Always made up stories. Always been able to imagine very vivid scenes from tiny actions in real life. Always been able to read people. Writing had always been his first language.

Dawn sent up a pink flush, a cock crowed and Mr Shakespeare stood up on his rickety ankles and creaking knees and set off through the crinkly, jack-frosted dew back to the ruins of the monastery. Somewhere in there Bethsabe was warming herself beside Uric and he tried not to let the thought hurt him. He could never be in love with her. It could never happen. It must never happen.

He ducked into his jagged-eye doorway and pushed aside the damp sacking. The small room he stepped into smelled of cheesy feet and soot and he nudged the figure under the mounds of old, moulding blankets until Romeo – for that was what the boy he'd found in the snow yesterday had said his name was – poked up his head and swore.

"Eat something and come to my room to begin your lessons," Will told him, not bothering to wait for a reply. Will was eager to teach: to actually teach someone something. "You've slept enough. If you want to stay here you must come to class. Idleness will do you no favours. We'll breakfast after."

Romeo arrived a few minutes later, white-faced and disorientated. Will had lit a fire and set out some books on the table before a wall. It was still dark out and two candles and the flames provided the only light in the room.

"I will instruct you in the ancient art of arguing *in utramque partem*," Will began.

"Latin?" sighed Romeo. *I'm in some terrible nightmare,* he thought. When he'd awoken that morning he'd felt sure he'd be with Gillian again. But he was here. In some kind of grimly realistic, stinking past.

Find out what's happening. Find her.

"Today you will learn to apply *inventio, dispositio, elocutio, memoria* and *pronuciatio*. You will learn to speak on both sides of an argument. You will see that any event – anything that happens to any of us – can be viewed, and written, from different perspectives."

Oh, I believe that, Romeo thought. *Oh, how I believe that.*

He concentrated on the lesson and enjoyed his work. He learned different tricks to create different effects. He might repeat something three times to make sure it worked, worked, worked. He might put two strange words together to say the work was enjoyably horrible. He might make all the words start or contain the same letter or sound to show that he'd studied several samples of variant styles to showcase what he wanted to demonstrate and was thus sated.

But behind it all, Romeo was planning on what he would say when he saw Gillian again. He didn't know where he was but he knew that if he had come here from wherever Gillian lived, there must be some way to get back there, or, at the worst, for her to get here. The fact that he was here meant there had to be some connection between the two places.

All was a dream – or nightmare – and the only thing real was the love he felt for Gillian. That was the only thing he could feel with all his heart and soul and the only thing in this whole mad episode which he felt he had some control over. The reality of their love, that vivid feeling, was more real than the school had been, certainly more real than the flashes of his old life he sometimes remembered; more real than this stinking, cold place.

Their love was his and Gillian's – no one else's. It was such a perfect love that it could never be something he'd invented. It was real. They were real. Love was real and this was a kind of test – a blackness, a vagueness which existed all around the warm sun that was at the heart of everything. This was a test, yes. He had been shown perfect love once and it was too perfect to be a lie. It was too wonderful. Too true.

"You smile?"

"I'm sorry, sir."

"Put the book down."

Romeo rubbed his eyes. He saw it was dark again, perhaps five or six in the afternoon. Twilight. He leaned back on the hard, wooden stool he used as a chair. Somewhere behind him his teacher was rummaging through a pile of books. "Why do you say your name is Romeo?" Will asked.

"Because it is, sir."

"Not your real name, though, is it?"

"I can't remember my real name, sir."

Will was holding a book to his chest. The boy had told him little or nothing as to how he had arrived, naked, at the school and Will had not pried. He knew the value of privacy and could tell that the boy had undergone some great mental upheaval. He thought perhaps he was a runaway – perhaps his whole family had been taken to heaven by the plague or religious zealots.

One never knew; one only knew not to ask too many prying questions. "Who calls you Romeo?"

The boy stared at the large granite stones ahead of him. "My one true love," he answered. His voice was a tone higher than usual, Will noticed. He was speaking from his heart.

"Does she live?"

"Yes. I hope."

"You know not?"

"For sure, no. The last I saw of her, yes. It's more likely she believes me dead."

Will guessed the young lovers had run into problems with the girl's family. Perhaps the girl was married. "Her name?"

"Gillian."

"Not Juliet?"

Romeo looked over his shoulder. "No. Why?"

"Since you've been so honest with me, I might as well be honest with you." Will took out the volume he was holding and passed it to Romeo. "I'm trained as a schoolmaster and I shall instruct you to the best of my abilities but my great ambition is to write for the stage." He watched the boy read the title.

"*The Tragicall History of Romeus and Juliet* by Arthur Brooke," Romeo read.

"It's poetry," Will explained. "A new version of an old story. Goes back as far as Xenophon of Ephesus. Old, old story. About lovers."

Romeo raised an eyebrow. "Only that? About lovers?"

"You should read it."

"What's your interest?"

Will shrugged his shoulders. "I'm writing a version of it. It would be interesting for me to know your opinion, seeing as you are so close to the subject. Sharing a name as you do. A story, certainly, although I hope it is not as tragic as theirs."

"Are you not in love yourself?"

Will thought about this a moment. "I'm too old," he said,

finally.

Romeo looked back at the book and then stood up. "I'll try it," he said. "I can't promise anything but I'll try it."

Will nodded. "Until the morrow, then."

"And yours?" Romeo asked, on the threshold. Behind him a gibbous moon was sliced by the misty night sky.

"My what, lad?"

"Your play?"

"Oh, I have some of it written, most of it here," Will replied, tapping a dirty finger to his temple.

Romeo shook his head and tapped his chest. "Should be here," he told his teacher. "In your heart."

Friday

1

Kizzie and Zak watched Gillian walk away into the foggy darkness which covered the playing fields. Far away, the windows of the Main Building floated like lights from a ghost ship. Although she tried to hide it, burying her head into the scarf she had wrapped around her face, it was obvious Gillian was crying.

"I don't get it," Kizzie said, turning to Zak and laying her head against his chest. They were at The Tree, the furthest point from the school they could be while still on the grounds. "It's not such a big deal."

"Are you serious?"

"What? A dinner and dance. What's the problem? It's not like we even have a choice about going or not going. We have to go."

"You really think she's worried about going?"

"Well, what's she worried about then?"

Gillian had now disappeared completely, eaten up by the fog.

"What's she worried about?" asked Zak, taking a step backwards. "She's worried about having to go with him. With Alain bloody Verne."

"So what? I still don't see the big deal. It's just business. Everyone's happy!"

"You're happy, you mean. You keep Verne happy, which keeps Fermin and the Magistrate off your back while poor Gillian gets hung out to dry."

"Why?" Kizzie faked exasperation. "What's so bad about going to a crappy dinner and dance with someone? It doesn't mean anything! It's not like she has to marry him!"

"She's already married!"

"Ha!"

"What?"

"Oh, come on, Zak."

"What?" Zak had a weird, steely look in his eye that seemed to affect the air around them. "Are you laughing at the wedding ceremony you presided over now?"

"Wedding ceremony?" Kizzie shook her head but there was no escape. She lifted her hands. "No. OK. I know they meant it, but come on. It wasn't like it was in a church. She just met the guy. And, besides, I told you, he wasn't even real. I knew that. I mean, what was I supposed to do? I was trying to make her happy."

"You're so cold sometimes," Zak said, backing away. He walked in small circles opening and closing a Zippo lighter he'd pulled from the pocket of his overcoat. "Why did you take me into the library to see The Book? You're like a criminal that keeps going back to the scene of the crime. You shouldn't act like you don't care, Kizzie, you haven't got the heart for it. Just be a nice person."

"Don't do that. Someone'll see us."

"So?" Zak lifted the lighter, popped the lid and sparked the flame.

"Very cool."

"At least tell me that somewhere you feel sorry for her."

"For who?"

"Who do you think? For Gillian! For what you did."

"Of course I do."

"She was in love with that guy, Kizzie."

"She'll get over it."

"Are you sure about that?"

Kizzie suddenly became as serious as Zak. "Of course I hate what I did – are you stupid? I just want everything to go back to normal. I want everything like it was. Who knows? Maybe she'll fall in love with Verne and they'll make the perfect couple and everything will be OK?"

"Where did they send him?"

"Verne?"

"Romeo." Zak raised an eyebrow as he said the name. "You know what, it doesn't matter how many times you say it, it still sounds weird."

Kizzie took her chance, smiled, and moved in again. Zak let her back into his arms. "I don't know where they sent him."

"And there's nothing you can do to get him back?"

Kizzie shrugged but she couldn't make herself say "no" out loud.

"Or send her there?" Zak sniffed. It was getting colder now by the second. "Just anything to get them back together."

"No!" said Kizzie.

Zak held her away from him. "No?" He looked right into her eyes. "That doesn't sound like a real 'no'."

"It's nothing."

"What?"

"No, seriously. Zak, no. Don't ask me this. Drop it." Kizzie walked away, her eyes wet and Zak watched her, surprised but weighing her up. Was she faking her emotion? The tears? He didn't think so.

"Wait." He caught up. Through the dense bracken and tree trunks, white and red lights slid by on the wet bypass. "Tell me."

"No." Kizzie was upset. She tried to cover her face with her hands. "Leave me alone, Zak. Seriously."

"Kizzie!" Zak turned her to him. "Tell me."

Kizzie struggled but Zak was strong and somewhere, deep down, she wanted to tell him. She wanted to tell him that there was a chance. A small chance. But the consequences of taking it – well, that she could never tell him. Everyone had their secrets, didn't they?

"There is something," Zak said.

"I don't know."

"What is it?"

"I don't think it would work."

"What? Kizzie! Tell me what."

James Hartley

Kizzie unzipped her jacket and reached down under her scarf and pulled up a small locket she had hanging around her neck on a gold chain. "There's a small scrap of paper in here. From The Book," she said. Just saying the words made her turn her head and look back in to the dark swirling mists. "It's only enough for a few words. One sentence. I kept it because..."

"If you write on it, you think it'll come true?"

"That's just it. I don't know." Kizzie wiped her tears with the back of her glove. "I just kept this in case I needed it. I didn't tell anyone."

Zak blew out a steady stream of air. "Do it," he said. "Send her to him. Get them back together."

Kizzie began crying. "But I don't know what that would mean. For her parents. Her family. I don't want to do this anymore."

"You did it when you were happy to do it," Zak told her sternly. "Now you should do it to clean up the mess. Send her to him and that's it. Let the rest take care of itself."

"But you don't know what that means," Kizzie said, bursting into tears, her face changing, crinkling up like a child's.

"I don't care!" Zak cried.

Kizzie rested a hand on his cheek and looked into her eyes, shaking her head sadly. Behind the tears her eyes sparkled and swam. "Oh, my poor baby."

Zak was thinking, *I'll never understand women.* "I don't get this, Kizzie. If you know something's right, you just have to do it."

"Just tell me you love me," Kizzie told him.

"And you'll do it?"

"Just tell me you love me. Hold me close, as tightly as you can, and tell me you love me and that you'll always love me, whatever happens."

"Why are you suddenly like this? What's up?"

"Because I waited so bloody long for you to come and now I need to hear it. I need to feel it!"

"But why now?"

"Just say it!"

Zak felt her shudder against his chest and he kissed her hair and told her he loved her and that he would always love her, whatever happened.

Instead of making her happy, though, this seemed to make Kizzie more upset. She cried hard, clinging to Zak as though her life depended on it.

2

'Tis *truly bleak midwinter*, Will thought as he trudged out into the snow. His toes were already numb although he'd stuffed blotting paper between his disintegrating socks and the well-worn leather.

The allotment plots were ridged and bare and the animal pens empty. Drifts had blown high up the wire fences and the pathway was black with ice.

Mrs Sharpe opened the door for Will but she was too tired to be rude, ushering him upstairs with little ceremony. The bottom floor was alive with animals and stunk. There was food and faeces on the floor but it was warm.

"Sir," Will said, pulling off his cap as he came up the last rung of the ladder and stood in the loft. He had to duck at the sloping roof and could smell something sweet and sickly, which might have been a tincture or ointment Mrs Sharpe had made or might just have been the smell of the old monk. The Master was lying on a low bed of straw in front of a window which glowed grey-silver from the snow falling between the black, bare fingers of the trees.

"Sharps-spear?"

"Will Shakespeare, sir. Yes, that's me." Will came over to the bed and it seemed only right to kneel.

The old monk looked shockingly ill and close to death. His face was very pale and lined with tiny red cracks; his nose purple and stained; his eyebrows and the hairs, which sprouted from his nose and ears, brilliantly white. His eyes were now completely pale blue, as though painted, and the sides of his mouth were very tight, as though drawn back on steel strings hidden somewhere behind his neck.

"Are you making progress with the boy?" the monk managed to say.

125

"I am, sir, I am." And Will did his best to ignore the monk's ravaged condition and spoke about his young pupil, about his Latin and learning.

"And you've been writing also?" the monk asked, when Will had finished.

"I have, I have." Will was rather startled to hear this and wasn't sure if it meant he was in trouble.

Later, when he remembered this scene, Will would never be sure quite how The Master had spoken to him, whether it had been with his own voice or whether he had simply thought the words aloud. There had been no doubting that words had passed between them, and that Will had heard them but, when he thought back, it seemed strange that a man in such bad condition would have been able to speak so eloquently and clearly. But all that was by the by. It had happened and it happened like this:

"You will be rich and famous, Will Shankspire."

"One lives in hope, sir."

"What you have learned here will cause your name to echo down through the ages. You will be famous across the land and across the world, in schools and on stages."

"I will be eternally grateful for your giving me a job here, sir. And for letting me use your magnificent library."

"Your fate will always be intertwined with ours, my young friend."

Will, who was kneeling, glanced up at The Master. The old monk was lying on his back, his eyes staring up at the termites quivering like white jelly in the low beams.

"How so, sir?"

"To leave your past behind and go to your bright future you must sign your name on the moon and watch it disappear."

Will stood up and leaned so close to the prone, dying man that he smelled again the tart, otherworldly smell he'd noticed when he'd entered the room. It was the old monk's breath. "I beg your pardon, sir? I don't understand."

"Sign your name on the full moon, Will."

"Sign my name on the moon?"

The monk reached out and laid his transparent hand on Will's own. The monk's skin was dead cold. "You will always be here with us, as will I. It is written. I have written it. You must write on the moon before you leave here – before you can leave here. A part of you will always be here with us, as will a part of me. Neither of us shall ever truly leave. Myself in spirit, you in words and deeds. Write on the moon and watch it disappear, Will. Write on the moon and watch it disappear to make the future bright."

Will shook his head. "I don't understand, sir."

"Ours is not to understand," the old monk replied, almost smiling. "You must realise this now, Will. We cannot understand everything. We are a part of everything and that is enough. It is not our place to understand. Understanding is beyond us, as it is all the animals, all the creatures, all of creation." The monk turned his head and as he began to cough a weird, yellow mixture, thick as custard but dotted with red globs, dripped out of his mouth and emerged from his nose to stain his filthy pillow. Spluttering, he managed to say, "I shall watch over you all. When I die, I will become the Guardian Spirit of this school, Will. So it is written, so it will come to pass."

"Shall I call for help, Master?"

"This school is my dream," the dying monk told him. "This is *my dream* you are in."

By now Will was alarmed by the old monk's condition. "I'm going to call Mrs Sharpe."

"No!"

"But, my Master, sir!"

"Promise me you will write on the moon, Will, and I will give you the stars!"

Will heard himself saying, "I will, sir. I will. But please let me go for help!"

Will's reply seemed to calm the old monk but he wouldn't let him go and beckoned the young man closer. When Will was so near to the man's face he felt physically sick at the smell, The Master whispered, "Take the book which is under my bed and hide it well. Hide it somewhere nobody will ever find it. Not for years."

"The book, sir?"

As Will turned his face to look at the monk, the dying man suddenly grabbed Will with the force of ten men. In a deep, terrifying voice, he screamed, "HIDE THE BOOK!" down Will's ear and dug his sharp, old, yellowing nails into the young man's shoulder, breaking the skin.

Will yelled out in pain and pushed the dying man away, standing stooped under the rafters as more vermillion vile slime seeped out of the old monk's ears, nose and mouth, while his pale blue eyes remained staring impassively up at the ceiling.

"Mrs Sharpe!" Will cried, throat filled with phlegm. "Mrs Sharpe!"

The yellow liquid pooled on the bed and began to drip down onto the dirty reeds and straw on the floor and, shaking, Will ran to the top of the ladder and shouted down, "Mrs Sharpe! Please come quickly!"

He ran back to the bed and was startled to see only the monk's cowl on the threadbare sheets. There was no sign of a body – no sign of The Master at all. Puddles of yellow slime shrunk and disappeared and the horrible smell faded away with the mess. Will leaned over the bed and unlatched the window and winter rushed into the room, snow with it, sniffing out every corner of the loft.

The Book.

Will crouched and looked under the bed. He saw a large, red, ledger-like tome and pulled it out, held it to his chest and crossed back to the ladder. At the foot of the steps he turned to see Mrs Sharpe standing in front of the fire with her hands buried in the front pockets of her apron. "Gone then, is he?" she asked.

"He is," nodded Will.

"You'd best be doing as you were instructed to, then, young man."

"Aye." Will pulled his hat on and let himself out into the falling snow. It was settling so quickly he couldn't see his own footprints but he walked out anyway, back towards the ruins, hoping, for once, he wouldn't see anyone before he'd had a chance to hide the book.

It was only when he was halfway across the white lawn, sloughing through snow, which sneaked up to his knees, that he realised all of the animals in the house had been dead calm when he'd come down the stairs and spoken to Mrs Sharpe. They'd all been standing as though stuffed: breathing, staring, very still.

Saturday

1

It began at twelve, on the stroke of midnight.

In Dorm Three the girls slept as Gillian slowly dissolved.

The steel frame of her bed seemed to fizz. The faded green duvet cover melted away into darkness. Kizzie snored, Angela dreamed and Priya muttered *no, no, no.*

Gillian felt nothing and soon she was gone: her clothes too, and the postcards of the kissing couple in Paris and a Helsinki Christmas market. In the laundry basket by the door her dirty clothes vanished and everything else slid down to take their place. Her shoes left only their dirt, in lines which crumbled under their own weight. Her fingerprint smudges smoothed over on the door handle and windowpanes. All traces of her evaporated, the atoms taking another shape, escaping, becoming something else.

Downstairs where the school photographs hung in frames around the walls, Gillian's image faded away. In some she was replaced, in others everyone was simply moved along. The first year she'd been there she'd been sitting cross-legged in the front row alongside Kizzie, both of them barely recognisable, both proudly sporting digital watches. In one of the later photos Gillian's face was scarred with spots and she had her chin tipped as low as she could, desperate not to be seen, not to be photographed. From these and more, her image slowly faded away.

In the staff room the name on Gillian's books, notes and folders morphed into other names in other people's handwriting, other fonts. In the school server her records changed, emails with her name were altered, her files reformatted. In the classrooms and library her name and initials and graffiti and notes dissolved, and a wet sock under a bush on the playing fields with her name sewn into it was eaten by a fox with naughty, glinting eyes.

A table in a piazza in a small town on an island off the Italian coast was empty, the waiter standing nearby in a white shirt and white waistcoat picking his teeth with a toothpick. Behind him, inside the bar, was a rowdy party. Mopeds buzzed by. Time moved so slowly he could watch the stars come out.

Fourteen years earlier, in the granite, lamp-lit streets of Aberdeen, a woman in a long raincoat and headscarf stepped into a pub, out of the lashing rain, and realised she'd come to the wrong place, the wrong pub. Instead of deciding to stay anyway and ask if she could use the telephone at the bar, she turned around immediately and went back out into the storm. She walked to the other pub, in the other street and met the man she'd been supposed to meet, her boss at the office. They would go on to have three children together, none of them Gillian.

Back in the first pub, sitting at the bar cursing his luck, a young businessman spun a fifty-pence coin on the wooden surface and thought about what he was going to do with his life. In another world, another time, a woman would have appeared at the bar beside him and asked to use the telephone. They would have started speaking and he would have charmed her and married her and they would have had Gillian three years from that very night. But now he span his coin, went back over the day's events and tried to work out what he should do. "Doug," he said. The fat barman with the bristly white moustache looked up from cleaning a glass.

"What's up?"

"Pass me the phone, will you?"

"There's a call box outside."

The man who might have been Gillian's father had sworn, slipped off his stool and walked out into the rain. In the red box he'd dialled a number on the back of the business card he had in his pocket.

"Mr Bryson?" he'd said. "I'd like to take the job after all."

And that's how he'd ended up sitting on the terrace of his

house in Australia thirteen years later with a can of *Fosters* in his hand, watching his three sons play cricket in the garden.

2

The body of The Master was cremated on a pyre in the corner of the school grounds that even at that time was called The Dips. The ground was marked by a series of ancient furrows and hollows where Viking boats might be buried, or which might have been the remains of a prehistoric settlement. It was a bleak, wintry afternoon.

In accordance with the Master's wishes, only Mrs Sharpe, Will and the three other teachers were in attendance. Mrs Sharpe watched sadly as the smoke and flames fought valiantly against the snow, which had been coming down, on and off, for most of the day. The pupils and villagers would pay their respects at a service at St Catherine's, which was scheduled for the next morning, weather permitting.

"Leave the body out tonight," Mrs Sharpe told Will as she crossed herself and made to leave. "It's what he wanted. What's then left by nature, gather up to be buried at the church tomorrow."

Will walked back to the ruined abbey with the proud, handsome Ayland, who looked as suave and sophisticated as ever, despite the weather. "You really shouldn't stay for too much longer, dear Will," the well-spoken young man was saying. "One of the tunnels is bound to collapse under the pressure of the snow before long. Why don't you come with me to town and stay a few days? Move on when the weather breaks? The pupils have been told to leave for their own safety. No reason why you shouldn't follow suit."

"I need to finish things."

"Ah." Ayland nodded. "The play, I presume?"

"Yes. Almost done. The quiet will do me good."

"Mind you don't get snowed in with it. That wouldn't do anyone any good."

"I won't. Plus –" Will gestured back towards the old house – "if I stay it'll give me a chance to keep an eye on Mrs Sharpe. Make sure she stays on an even keel."

"Very thoughtful of you." Ayland stopped at the dark doorway. "Will you be joining us again next term? We'll have The Quad mapped out by then. Work should start as soon as the flowers pop up."

"I don't think so," Will answered. Voicing this thought made him both embarrassed and sad. He was slightly ashamed that The Master, Ayland and the others had taken him in, taken him under their wings, only for him now to go running away from them, but he also knew it was what he had to do.

"Don't worry. We didn't expect you to remain here for long, you know." Ayland touched Will's cheek. "Ulric is going too. He's never been content here."

"Oh, but I have been happy. I'm only sorry that my departure has to be so abrupt."

"We'll always be thankful for the work you've done in the library."

"A pleasure, really. It's all been a pleasure. It's just sometimes you feel you have to move on, I suppose. I feel I have to go."

"We'll always have your plays, eh?"

Will reddened. "I hope so. For what it's worth."

"We know so," nodded Ayland, and both men ducked inside the ruined abbey. "In fact, I have something to ask you about that, Will."

"Oh, yes?"

"A rather delicate matter, I'm afraid. Money. Sorry to be so vulgar."

Will shook his head. "Don't worry. My position on that is simple: I have none."

"And I much." Ayland watched Will.

"Aye, well, some of us are lucky, I suppose."

"Luck has nothing to do with it. It's all about land, Will.

About owning things."

"One does not choose where one is born on this globe, Ayland, where one 'pops up', as it were. I didn't choose my life and you didn't choose yours. 'Twas luck, or something like it, that's all. One makes the best of what is given."

This little speech caught both men by surprise. Will felt as though he had spoken his thoughts out loud and shocked himself by going on. "I like to think that it doesn't bother me where I was born, you know. If I'd been rich, I would have been rich. If I were poor, I would have been poor. As it is, I'm somewhere in the middle, sometimes rich, sometimes poor. Be that as it may, I'm a writer and the world is my subject. I simply write what I see as I hope I would if I were richer or poorer."

"Very noble." Ayland nodded. "But you must want for an audience, surely?"

"I do of course."

"And that's what I'm saying." Ayland patted Will on the shoulder. "That's how I can help you, you see."

"My brains and your money?"

"Our brains and my money," Ayland replied, laughing. "What say you?"

"Sounds good."

"Shall I have someone draw up a contract or shall we shake upon it? *Shake*speare?"

Will smiled and held out his hand. "We shall do both. In this handshake, my agreement. In the contract, the details."

Will had the strange feeling, as he shook hands with the tall boy, that he was part of someone else's plan, playing a role in a great drama that he would never quite understand. It was almost the same as it had been with the Master: as it had been with everything at the school. Some places on earth had a magic and spirituality to them which was almost tangible, he felt, and this was one of them. He sensed it all around him, in the ruins and in the people. He felt it in Ayland. Perhaps it was simply charm, a kind of chemical magic. It was seductive, though, whatever it was, and Will wanted to believe in it.

"Will?"

Turning at the top of the narrow staircase down which Ulric and now Ayland had already descended, Will looked behind himself into the shadows and saw Bethsabe with a shawl wrapped around her shoulders, holding out her hand to him.

"Quick. Come here!"

"But?"

"Please, don't argue. Come here!"

Will went across to where Bethsabe was, ducking under the heavy, hanging tapestry she'd lifted, and found himself in a small room littered with great cubes of hewn stone lit by candles. The walls had been decorated with chalk or charcoal, not images but patterns, and Will knew instinctively that Bethsabe had made the designs.

"I wanted to say goodbye," she told him, taking his arm to pull him towards her as he examined the swirls on the ceiling.

Will looked back at the fabric door. Ulric was never far away from Bethsabe. Will and Bethsabe hadn't spoken to each other since the day in his room, if indeed that had ever happened. They were never alone. Only via their eyes had they communicated; or lying in bed at night, apart, together in each other's minds – but then one never knew if any of that were true either. "Are you leaving?" he asked.

"No. I thought you were. I heard you saying goodbye to Ayland."

"No, no. I'm staying here a while. Until I finish my work." He had never been this close to her: her soft, caramel face, so perfectly curved, was all he could see. Her eyes were a deep, soothing brown, with flashes of amber. "Why do you ask?"

Her face hardened. "I didn't want you to go without saying goodbye."

Will looked down at their hands. She had taken hold of his

and he felt a current pass between them; it brought guilt and pleasure. "We shouldn't be in here together, Bethsabe. If Ulric comes..."

She took a step forwards, her nose just below his. "He's leaving."

"So Ayland says."

"I am alone here. Like you."

"I'm married!"

"You left your wife, Will!"

"But I am married!"

"Do you love her like you love me?"

"I will not answer that, Bethsabe." Will broke apart and stepped back.

"Because you know it is not true! It's our love that's true. You profess to love truth, yet you run from it. You run from me. You run from love."

"I feel a duty."

"Your only duty is to the truth and love!" She placed a hand on his shoulder and rubbed her hand down his back. "Your duty now is to me. To us."

"If I give myself to you, you may destroy me."

"So? Let us both burn in the fire of our love! Turn around, Will. Kiss me. Kiss me like you want to. Stop fighting what you know is right."

And she pulled him around and clasped him close to her body and they kissed and it was as wonderful as he had dreamed it would be.

3

Kizzie woke up just after two in the morning. Priya was coming back from the toilet with a dead-eyed look on her face. On any other day this might have been comical but after a deep sleep, in the chilly midnight shadows, it creeped Kizzie out. "Are you all right?" she asked as her friend stood stock still inside the dorm, at the door, holding the handle.

Priya didn't, or wouldn't, reply and Kizzie was caught in two minds. Was Priya sleep walking? Weren't you not supposed to wake a sleepwalker? Wasn't it dangerous?

Just as Kizzie was thinking about getting up, Priya turned and walked across to her bed, pulling the rustling duvet over her body in a single movement. A few mutters and sighs later and she was snoring.

Kizzie turned to the wall, aware that she was wide awake – all she could think of was Gillian – and concentrated on the firework shapes in the darkness on the back of her eyelids. Behind her, above Priya, the bunk bed Gillian had slept in was gone, the wall bare. Nobody had said anything that night as they'd gone to bed, not Angela, Priya or any of the other girls who'd come and gone in the noisy hour before lights out.

Gillian had simply never been to the school.

I'll think of her like I think about grandma, Kizzie thought. Kizzie's grandmother had died when she was ten years old and she had a better relationship with her now than she'd ever had when the old lady was alive.

Kizzie shook her head and said, *I'm sorry, Grandma. Sorry for what I've done*. She often spoke to her grandmother as others might speak to their god.

For a terrible moment, eyes clenched shut, Kizzie thought that even her grandmother was going to forsake her but then she noticed a bright light, like an indistinct sun, shining through the darkness of the back of her eyes. Blinking them open she saw a glow on the bobbled wall in front of her face and turned slowly over to face the dorm. What she saw made her stomach contract with shock.

In the centre of the room, a cowled monk with bright blue eyes was hovering above the shiny floor. The monk looked impossibly old. His skin was drawn and wrinkled as though he were made of paper and had been folded in a box for thousands of years. As Kizzie stared, he raised a finger and she heard the words:

You know what you have done.

You know what remains to be undone.

Kizzie whispered, "I'm sorry" in the most pathetic voice she'd used in years. It was her childhood voice, her homesick voice, her helpless voice – a voice which had long since been taken over by a more confident, slightly arrogant tone.

Not knowing what else to do, Kizzie lifted both hands above the sheets and pressed them together in prayer and as she did so the monk seemed to smile, bowed his head and slowly disappeared, fading away with the light.

The tight ball of nerves in Kizzie's stomach told her what she'd seen hadn't been a dream or vision. The horrible, wide-eyed realisation that nothing was ever going to be the same again announced itself and she lay there wide awake, thinking on the monk's words, trying, in her mind, to make this all somehow not her fault, not her doing. What she really wanted, and not for the first time, was a rewind button. Oh, for a rewind button, to zip backwards in time and not do what she had done!

But there was no way out. She had made all this happen.

She lay awake for hours and hours with no escape from herself.

The worst, she knew, was yet to come.

"Oh my God, Kizzie, what's the matter with you? You look

terrible!"

"I don't know." Kizzie shook her head. "Bad sleep. Nothing."

"I feel yuck too, today." Angela was pulling hard on the laces of her sport's shoes.

"Why? What's up with you?" Priya asked Angela. Priya was standing in front of the mirror with two pink hair clips poking out of her mouth.

Angela leaned against her bedside cabinet to stretch her calves. "I dunno. I just feel like I'm going mental."

Kizzie was buttoning up her school shirt. Part of her was happy Angela was not feeling well. It made her feel less awful about feeling horrible herself. But as soon as she thought this, she talked to herself. *Don't make this worse than it is.*

"Tell us, then," Priya was saying.

"It's that bloke. The Shakespeare bloke."

"You saw him again?"

Kizzie glanced over at Priya and thought how bright the wall looked where Gillian's bunk should have been. Right about now Gil would have been peeping her head over the duvet and moaning about the light or the time.

"It's got to be an actor or someone who's like a fan or something," Priya said. "Someone from the village. Amateur dramatics or something. Some of the Year Nine girls dress up as me. It's normal."

"No, but –" Angela scrunched her face up – "I don't think it's normal, you know. I don't think it's something I should have seen."

"What? Like a ghost?" asked Priya in the reflection. She smacked her lips. God, she was gorgeous.

Angela shrugged. "Maybe." She wanted to tell them a few things she was known for in her family but they were subjects you couldn't just blurt out. Stories about how she'd had invisible friends when she was little. About how she'd once told her mother about a previous life she remembered. Stuff that had faded away as she'd got older. Things that now made no sense and couldn't possibly be true. "Ah, it's nothing."

"Why don't you speak to someone?" Priya asked. "If it's doing your head in you should talk to someone."

"Talk to Leana," Kizzie said. She knotted her tie and tried to smile but all the life and hope had been sucked out of her. It was true that morning – daylight – had improved things but the knot in her stomach was still there and the normality of the day, the humdrum routine of the morning, made everything hurt.

She felt like a ghost must, when they realise they're a ghost. How sweet are all the normal, boring things we take for granted when you can't have them? Friends. Chit-chat. The view from the window and nothing to worry about but the usual stuff?

"I tried," said Angela. She stood up. Her face was very pale from the cream she'd used for her spots.

Kizzie was surprised. Angela was usually closed to suggestions. "And?"

"She ignored me."

"Try again!" said Kizzie. "She's the one you have to talk to. Seriously. Just ask her again."

Angela looked shy. "I don't know."

Priya held Angela's hand. "You do look so tired."

"I'm all right," Angela replied. "I'm just trying to work out what it all means. A run'll help."

"Coming, Kiz?" asked Priya, and the three of them left the dorm, which smelled of shampoo and wet towels and aerosol sprays, and walked out into the corridor.

The heaters were on and girls passed by in the opposite direction, some in bathrobes, some in PE kit and others heading the same way, to the main staircase and down to breakfast.

Kizzie dropped behind the other two when they got to the queue for the breakfast hall. She looked over the shoulders of the children in front of them and saw, through the steamed-up window, Zak laughing with Sol at their usual table. Kizzie's eyes watched Zak's until her boyfriend looked up at her, caught her eye, and winked. He held up a pen drive and waved it and she forced herself to smile as the door opened and the Consul let in the next six children.

Kizzie was cut off from Priya who made it through into the warmth – she pressed her hands and nose against the glass from inside the door like a prisoner – but there was nothing the Consul was going to do to change his mind. He was a big, burly sixth former with stubble and a double chin who went back to his mobile phone without even acknowledging Kizzie's protestations.

"Kizzie?"

Kizzie turned and got a shock as she saw Alain Verne. "Oh, hello."

"May we have a chat?"

He looked the same as ever. Recovered, but ever so slightly wild about the eyes.

"Ah, it's just – you know. Breakfast." Kizzie shrugged and pointed at Priya who immediately looked up and, for some reason, whistled. "I need food. I didn't sleep well."

Alain leaned in to her ear. "Did you enjoy your visit from The Master last night?"

"Who?"

The Consul leaned back and opened the door as his phone bleeped with an incoming message but Kizzie was paralysed.

"Our friend the monk," Alain said, in a too-loud voice, but nobody around them seemed to pay any attention.

"Are you coming in or out?" asked the Consul.

"What do you want?" Kizzie asked Verne.

"Help."

"No."

"I think both of us need some help, and quickly." He stared into her eyes and Kizzie could hear the good part of her screaming, *Forget it! Go into the dining hall! You're in enough trouble as it is!*

"In!" Kizzie shouted, squeezing inside and watching the door close between her and Alain Verne.

4

Angela ran out along her normal route and felt the usual tension in her calves and thighs as her cold body strained to wake up. Her mind was fully awake. Like Kizzie, she'd hardly slept.

She looked down at the hard, dry pebbles on the path. Sometimes there were puddles here, sometimes even puddles filled with tadpoles. Now everything was rather dull, like the sky, although at least it wasn't raining.

She ran past the ponies in their field, swishing tails and ears against the flies, and wondered, as usual, if she would prefer to change places with them. Did they know they were stuck in a field? Probably. Did they know that if they leapt the low wooden fence and the two strings of electrified wire, they would be free? Probably.

But then she always remembered a day at home, years ago, when she was seven or eight, and a friend of hers had told her to let the canary they had out of the cage and they'd opened the small door and beckoned the creature out, to fly away, to escape (even if it would have only been around the living room). The small, yellow bundle had remained cowering at the back of its perch, in the farthest corner of its cage, shaking with fear.

Angela came out over the gravestones and soft mossy grass of the churchyard and looked up at the hills. Today she could see them in brilliant detail, all the different hues of the leaves and the dark, gnarled shapes of the branches and trunks. She breathed in the greenness and thought, *everything is going to be all right today*. Perhaps it was only the night. When you woke up in the night everything you'd been thinking of in the dead of night, alone, seemed exaggerated, didn't it? Your mind made connections that seemed silly when illuminated by daylight.

But what about the man? Go on, Angela – say it: *What about William Shakespeare?*

Well, of course it wasn't Shakespeare. It was just some man wandering about the hills, lost. Perhaps the bloke had some kind of mental illness? Perhaps he was someone who dressed like Shakespeare, or people of that time. An actor, like Priya had said. Or maybe those sort of clothes were back in fashion for some people? Whatever it was, he was not someone who had lived and died over four hundred years ago because that sort of thing just didn't happen. It was impossible.

But, she thought, heading up the steep, winding, woody path towards The Gallops, maybe she would still try to talk to Leana again. It wasn't just the Shakespeare thing – it was everything. Angela had been feeling strange recently. A lot of things she'd thought she'd liked were now odd to her, childish, even. Her body was changing: her face the most obvious thing to the outside world, but that was just one of her worries. Too many other, odd things. Strange new thoughts. She had started noticing the look in people's eyes: people looking at her in a different way, with different intentions.

And she trusted Leana. Leana was one of those people who seemed to understand everything. She'd heard the stories about her, but instead of scaring her, they only made Leana seem more real to her. Angela didn't really feel that with anyone else, not anyone older than herself. Miss Bainbridge hardly noticed her, and when she did, she spoke to her like a child. In class she never met the teacher's eye, for different reasons, face down in a book or face burning with potential shame at having to talk out loud. Her new greatest fear was that she would have to stand up in class and speak and that everyone would stare at her. Whenever she spoke to more than one person these days, Angela went to pieces.

She ran along The Gallops and looked down at the bypass and, beyond, the lovely sunlit expanse of the playing fields and the school. It really was a gorgeous spot on mornings like this and Angela was happy she was there. She would have been like this anywhere, she knew, confused and strange. Here she was allowed out to run and people left her alone. At the moment she could control her thoughts and no one really knew what she was thinking and that's how she liked it.

But now, beginning to head downhill, she couldn't help but think of the man. Say it! *Of William Shakespeare.*

But she didn't see him.

She expected him to pop out from behind the tree trunks or be standing in front of her on the narrow, winding dirt path but he never was and she got down to the bypass thinking: *That's it, it's over. Whatever it was, it was all in my head and that's it. Finished.*

But then she noticed that the cars passing her by were largely silent. There was only the faint hum of wind and some sort of motor, a faint buzzing, like a bulb, as each vehicle passed by.

Closer inspection revealed that each car – they were sleek, creamy, silvery designs, all of them, like small jets – had no drivers. Most of the windows were tinted and opaque but sometimes she caught sight of a person in the backseat and strange lights flickered from their eyes.

A child – a girl – looked out at her, a metal-looking, claw-like hand pressed to the window, and it was only when she'd gone that Angela realised the girl had been completely bald.

5

"What the hell did Verne want?" Sol Kerouac asked Kizzie as she and Priya came over to the boy's table.

"Nothing." Kizzie wanted to sit next to Zak but had no choice but to take a seat on Zak's far side, near the window, opposite her sister Athy. The seat next to Sol was saved for Priya. He had his cigarettes and lighter on it.

As Priya sat down she took out her chewing gum long enough to kiss Sol, both of them with eyes tightly closed, tongues fighting, before popping it back in her mouth and chewing again.

"So is that it, you two?" Zak asked. "Is it official now? Are we going to see some serious Facebook updating today?"

"Believe in love now, do we, Zak?" Kizzie asked.

"Where's your mate Angela?" Sol asked, chewing toast with his mouth open. "Pointlessly running around and hallucinating?"

"Don't be mean, Sol," Athy piped up.

"Oh! The dormouse speaks!" Sol said. He put his arm around Priya and squeezed her. "Missed you, babe."

"I'm not in the mood for you being nasty," Kizzie told Sol.

"Oh, big sister stands up for little sister. That's cute."

Kizzie swore, something she usually didn't do, and whipped her tray around to the table behind her. Two boys who were hunched up together playing on a small device looked up in horror, thinking she was a teacher. "Chill," she told them.

"You're not going to tell?"

"No, no." Kizzie looked down at her very dry scrambled egg and poked the hard, yellow mound with her fork. The rim of her green, steaming tea mug looked as if a toddler had been using it to soothe their teething pains. The tray under the mug and plate was greasy and the noise in the dining hall was horrendous.

"Are you all right?" Zak asked, placing a hand on her shoulder.

"Yes," Kizzie replied. "No."

"Can I do anything?"

"No, no. Just leave me alone. I'll be fine. Give me ten minutes."

"All right. Sure?"

"Sure?"

"Just realised you look like a sheep?" Sol shouted from the middle of the hall where he was waiting for Zak. Kizzie flipped him the finger and gritted her teeth. Why did Sol have to be like that? What did Priya see in him? When Kizzie had asked her, the reply had been, "He's such a man." As if that excused everything. But then, Kizzie couldn't help thinking that there was one of the problems between men and women summed up in one, clear example. A pretty girl like Priya, who could have any man she wanted (not that she needed to have any man), chose the biggest, most aggressive beast of the group.

It's nature, she almost heard Sol say.

Well, I don't like aggressive, horrible, alpha, King Kong idiots, she replied in her mind.

"Priya left her phone," Athy said, come around to sit opposite her sister. "I've got two exams today, can you believe that?"

"Really?" Kizzie looked up and sympathised. "Have you revised?"

"More or less." Athy couldn't help looking at the screen of Priya's phone. She wasn't allowed her own yet. "I don't get this thing of having the weather on your phone. Can people not just look out of the window?"

"People like reading it on their phones." Kizzie pushed away the plate. Her stomach felt as though it had shrunk. She couldn't eat.

"But it's crazy. Mr Yahudi was telling us that these days Facebook and Google and people like that know more about us than we do. They can read your mails, you know, see what you buy, what you like, process all this information."

"Big data." Kizzie yawned. "Oh God, when are the holidays?"

"I keep hearing that, but I don't get it. What is it? Big data?"

"It's everything. It's information. All the information about everything you do."

"So?"

"So that's how they know about you."

"So?"

"So –" Kizzie shrugged – "I don't know. So they can sell you things. Know what you're doing. Guess where you're going to go, where you're going to be. Bad stuff, I guess."

"But how can they know what I'm going to do if I don't even know what I'm going to do?" Athy asked. "That's dumb."

"You think you're in control of your own life?" Kizzie said aloud. It was really a rhetorical question. "I think the idea that you have any control over your own life is dumb."

"Oh, soh-ree. What's up with you today?"

Kizzie stared at Athy but she couldn't say anything. What could she say? "Ah, nothing. Ignore me."

"Yeah, well, I have to go." Athy slid Priya's phone across the table towards Kizzie. "Give this to P when you see her."

Kizzie looked down at Sol's grinning, gormless face. "Oh God."

The bell rang and Kizzie knew she had to get up, drop off her tray and move on to the next activity. *This is like prison*, Kizzie thought. *This is so like prison*.

But if you'd have asked her she wouldn't have known if she was talking about the school or her life.

6

"Angela?"

Angela opened her eyes and saw Leana.

The Head Girl had long, dark hair, parted in the centre, just like her own, which always looked marvellously clean, unlike her own. Angela thought the other girl had a weird, woollen, housey smell, which reminded her of the Senior Girls dorms in the boarding house she'd only ever been into once. It made her stomach feel funny and she backed up against the headboard, slightly overwhelmed by Leana being right then, on the edge of her bed, so close.

"I can come back later?"

"No, no."

Angela sat up. She noticed she was still wearing her running gear, her muddy trainers on a stool behind Leana. She was in Sick Bay, the curtains drawn, the radiators humming. It was warm and balmy. There was a sink in the room and, on the floor, an old telephone you had to use your finger to dial with, its cord wrapped around the base.

"Do you remember anything?" Leana asked. As she spoke her own phone buzzed and she looked down, checked the message, and then turned it off. "Sorry. Go on."

Angela was thinking about the cars: about the girl in the car with the metal hand against the window. "I don't know. What happened to me?"

"You fainted on the pavement by the bypass."

"Fainted?"

"Do you eat before you run, Angela? The other girls said you normally have breakfast when you come back."

"I prefer to run on an empty stomach."

Leana pursed her lips. "Oh, come on. That can't be good for you."

"I've always done it."

"Yes, but you've not always run as much as this, have you?"

Angela shrugged. "Maybe not."

"What are you training for now?"

"Nationals."

"Wow."

"It's not, you know, *that* exciting. I'm not that good."

"Oh, I don't think that's true."

Angela propped herself up on her pillows. "Can I ask, miss – I mean, Leana – can I call you Leana?"

"Of course."

"Can I ask why you're here? I mean – have you been talking to someone? The girls, you said, just now. Do you mean Kizzie and Athy? Priya?"

"Priya." Leana nodded. "She told me everything. I know all about the strange man."

A blush broke out over Angela's face and neck. "Oh God."

Leana reached out and touched her hands which were folded on top of the sheets. "You're not mad."

"I tried to tell you before."

Leana leaned forwards and took Angela's hands, which shocked the other girl. "I know, I know and I'm sorry." She let Angela withdraw her hands and waved her own. "Sorry, I didn't mean to startle you. I'm just so sorry. It's been a really tough few weeks for you from what I can gather."

Angela, her mind in turmoil, rolled her eyes. "So, what? It's real, is it? He's real?"

"Maybe."

"I didn't see him this time."

"This morning, you mean?"

"Uh-huh."

"But you're pretty sure you saw him before?"

"I think so."

"Well, for what it's worth, I think you did too."

"You've seen him?"

"Not him." Leana blew a jet of breath up into her fringe. "But I've seen things. Things that other people haven't seen. Can't see."

"Am I mad?"

"If you're mad, I'm mad," Leana replied.

"I feel mad."

Leana examined Angela. She was a strange creature, in the middle of a kind of metamorphosis between her girlish self and the woman she'd become. Her face was spotted red, her long hair was greasy and her body was too thin and wiry. She was changing, changing everywhere, physically and mentally. "You're at a very important time in your life, Angela," Leana told her. "A lot of things are happening to you, and around you, and you're very sensitive to everything. Pain hurts you a lot more than it ever has done before. You get very happy sometimes - too happy really. It can be hard to really know what you're thinking because what you're thinking seems to change so quickly."

Angela's eyes were now locked on Leana's. "You some kind of mind reader, too?"

"No," shrugged Leana, smiling. "I've been there, that's all."

"Sometimes everything makes sense."

"The most sensitive part of you is now very near the surface, Angela," Leana said. "That means you're picking up on everything, noticing everything, feeling everything. But you can also get hurt very easily. You are unprotected right now. You're like a snail that's come popping out of her shell."

"I just want to get back in it."

"I know, and you will. You will." Leana took off the green cardigan she was wearing and folded it over her knees. "One day you'll look back on this time as special, which is strange, I know. But you'll never feel some emotions quite so deeply again."

"Ugly is what I feel," Angela said, closing her eyes. "I look like a freak."

"You don't." Leana shook her head.

"I've got weird ears. And feet. Ridged nails. Spots in my nose and throat, even on my eyelids. Fat ankles even if I don't eat." Angela stopped. She knew she was going too far. Telling all her secrets.

"Haven't they explained to you what's happening, Angela? Your body is changing. Everyone goes through this."

"I saw flying cars," Angela declared quietly, her eyes clenched closed. "On the bypass. I guess that's why I fainted. I saw flying cars with no drivers. And some people, in the backseats, looked like robots, maybe, or half-robots. And I saw a girl who waved at me. She had a metal hand. I think that was the end. That was when I fell over, fainted or whatever."

After a long pause, Leana replied, in a calm voice, "It sounds like you saw the future this morning instead of the past."

Angela opened one eye. She did indeed have a spot on the inside of one eyelid, a painful little volcano which hurt every time she blinked. "What?"

"That's what I think happened. You saw the future. A future. Some variant of it."

"How could I see the future? That's impossible."

"You saw a version of the future, I said. Your future, perhaps. Or a future someone here has written." Leana said this as if reminding Angela to do up her shoelaces.

Angela was getting a glimpse into a side of Leana – and the school – which she'd heard about from time to time, late at night, in whispers, in corners, but had hoped was exaggerated. "What can I do to stop seeing this stuff?"

"Have you been tested?"

"Yes. I think so. Same as everyone else."

"Hmm." Leana bit her thumb. "Do you have any brothers and sisters here?"

"No. Just me."

Leana shrugged. "Maybe you're going to develop The

Power," she said.

"Oh God."

"Oh, it's not that bad. You'll be trained. Instructed. Guided."

"I don't want to see that sort of stuff all the time."

"Do you write? Stories? Poems?"

"No! Nothing! I've got no imagination!"

"Impossible." But Leana thought about things. "It could be interference." She leaned across and touched the back of her hand against Angela's forehead. "The pill you took is working. How do you feel? See if you can stand up." She helped Angela out of bed.

"So none of that stuff existed?" Angela asked. Her thin, Bambi legs were wobbly, splattered with dry mud, but after a quick stretch she felt life returning. "The cars and that?"

"No, no. They did exist."

"Shakespeare and the cars were real?"

"Oh, yes."

Angela stared at Leana in horror. "I'm lost."

"Oh, goodness me, come on." Leana placed both hands on Angela's shoulders. "Have you ever had a dream?"

"A dream?"

"Yes, at night. Or in a class." Leana giggled. "Anywhere. A dream. Haven't you ever dreamed?"

"Yes, of course I have."

"Did it exist?"

"What? The dream?"

"Yes."

"Did it happen, do you mean?"

"Yes."

"Yes. Of course. But not the stuff in the dreams."

"Sure?"

Angela thought about this. "Sure."

"What about movies? Ever seen a film?"

Angela pulled a *don't be silly* face. "Come on."

"Enjoyed it?"

"Some."

"Did they happen?"

"What? The stuff in the films?"

"Was there any moment when you believed what was going on?"

"Yes – of course."

"Are you here now? Talking to me?"

"What? Yes!"

"Sure?"

7

Ever since breakfast Kizzie had been nervous about Alain Verne accosting her but somehow she'd managed to put it out of her mind. She made it through Assembly, noticing him briefly out of the corner of her eye, and made sure she left the hall in a great crowd of people.

She walked up to lessons with Priya and Athy and thought – *it's strange that I don't miss Gil* – but she also knew that not missing her was all part of it. Gillian had disappeared from their lives as though she had never been there. All the feelings had gone too.

Kizzie hoped Gillian was somewhere else, happy: happy with her Romeo. As she walked up the steps to The Quad, she tried to imagine what that place was like, but all she could think of was a kind of summery heaven with lots of green fields, a blue sky and rainbow. There were hills stretching right out to the bright distant horizon and people were jumping about being infinitely happy until infinity. With this odd vision in her head, Kizzie thought, *Oh, I hope Gillian's heaven is better than that.* She couldn't really imagine Gillian fitting in somewhere like that, let alone Romeo.

And besides, if she was in heaven, wouldn't that mean she was dead?

The class stood in a huddle outside Room Four and Zak sidled over to Kizzie and asked her if she wanted to go fishing at lunchtime. Kizzie pulled a face. "Fishing? What are you on?"

"It's the perfect day for it," Zak said. "Down to the river, socks and shoes on the bank. Just us. Come on!"

"We're not allowed out of the school."

"Since when's that bothered you?"

"I don't have a rod."

"We'll make one."

Zak leaned in so close to Kizzie's ear that when he spoke it tickled. "I need to talk to you. Away from here. About things." He drew his face back and Kizzie saw some emotion there that she hadn't seen before. It might have been fear. "Important stuff."

"OK."

All around them the others filed into the classroom and Kizzie saw Zak's face change again, lighten and brighten and go back to normal, and the class walked into the chilly room. The teacher, Mrs Smith, told them to put on the heating and gradually they settled down to Venn Diagrams. Nobody mentioned Gillian but Kizzie was starting to get used to no one mentioning Gillian. She realised with horror she was starting to wonder if Gillian had ever been there at all.

Mrs Smith was a good teacher and the class behaved. A kind of calm trance of learning took over everyone in the room and any passer-by would have looked in to see bowed heads and a pretty, autumnal scene through the windows in the opposite wall. It was a clear day – not quite sunny, but light and airy and promising – and the trees were honey-brown and the leaves crispy yellow. Occasionally a leaf would flutter down to the ground to join its fallen comrades and squirrels darted along the boughs, straightening up, chewing and twitching before arrowing off again, bushy tails following behind like separate animals.

"Kizzie?"

Kizzie looked up and saw Alain Verne standing next to Mrs Smith.

"You're wanted."

Kizzie couldn't do much but pack up her things, hoist her bag up onto her shoulder and follow Alain out. As they came out into the cold air of The Quad, the Head of the Magistrate said, "After you. I want to keep an eye on you this time."

"Where are we going?" Kizzie asked as they approached the

steps.

"Formally, we're going to sign your resignation papers," Alain replied. He had an expensive looking scarf knotted in the continental style over his blue school duffel coat. His eyebrows had been plucked. Every individual blonde hair in the quiff, which rose up from his shining forehead, was visible. His cheeks shone and his eyes had a black dot of concentration in the centre of the pupils. "Informally, you're going to give me back what you've taken away."

Kizzie followed Verne around the Main Building. His cologne was faintly girlish. From behind you noticed his size, that he was shorter than most of the other boys his age despite his broad, weights-bulked shoulders. Come what may, he couldn't hide his height behind uniform or rank. "I don't get it, Alain, sorry. What exactly did I take from you?"

"Gillian," the boy replied curtly.

Kizzie followed him in through the back door and, without any fuss or attempt at hiding what they were doing, they walked straight down the corridor to the Eleusinian Room. Alain had a key, which he used, locking the door behind them as they moved into the greenish darkness. Two high ceiling lights flickered on and dust motes moved in the light beams criss-crossing the empty room. The library ladder was folded up, the flags were hanging as limply and sadly as always, and there was a faint smell of new paint in the air.

"You will send me wherever you sent her," Alain began. He unhooked a stepladder and unfolded it downwards, grimacing as he almost caught his fingers in one of the metal joints. It slid down to the floor with a clank.

"I don't know where she is."

"No matter. Just send me to wherever you sent her."

Kizzie looked back at the door. "If you're expecting me to write, I can't. I don't have the power. They've taken it away."

"They can't," Alain replied, huffing as he extricated The

Book. There was speed and precision in his movements. He knew what he wanted to do and came back down the ladder with ease, despite his load. "They can block you and they can stop you and they can make it difficult for you but they can never take away The Power. They didn't give it, they don't understand it and they can't do anything about it." He stopped, having flipped open the book on a teak table, and unclipped the top of a cheap ballpoint pen. "But I can use it. Perhaps to both of our benefits. Come here."

"What do you want me to do?" asked Kizzie. She kept her distance.

"I told you and I warn you, I will not tell you again. Send me to wherever you sent her."

"Who?"

"Come here now."

"No!"

"Come here now! You are in no position to argue."

"Why should I help you? I've got nothing to gain from this." Kizzie took a step forwards and there were tears in her eyes. "I'm sick of all this. Nothing good can come of this. I don't owe you anything. I don't owe anyone anything. I made a mistake and I've been punished and that's it."

Alain seemed angry and he looked as though he were about to shout. But he controlled himself. Counted to ten. Stared at the floor. Looked up. "The monk you saw this morning, Kizzie. Do you know who he is?"

"No."

"We both know there is another person here who shouldn't be here, don't we? Someone *you* created. Someone who has to go back to where they come from."

Kizzie stopped crying. "What are you talking about?"

"The Master knows everything. The Master knows what is real and what's not. He is in charge of removing people he knows are not real." Alain sighed. "There's nothing to be done now, Kizzie, except to help me. What's done is done."

"I don't understand why I have to help you."

"Because I can get you the time you need."

Kizzie looked into the prefect's eyes and saw he was telling the truth. "How long?"

"Enough."

Kizzie sighed. "And if I don't?"

"Then we'll both walk out of here and you'll find that you're completely alone. You'll never get the chance to say goodbye to your creation. You'll always regret not writing one simple sentence."

After a moment's hesitation, Kizzie walked across to the book, took the pen and wrote what Alain told her to write. When she'd finished she closed the heavy covers and straightened up. Before she turned around she knew Alain had gone, but also that she was not alone.

"Who's there?"

In the bottle-green shadows under the steel library scaffolding a figure walked forwards. It was the monk she had seen in her bedroom that morning, hooded, cowled, shuffling with an irregular, painful-looking gait. "You have shown compassion, my dear."

Kizzie saw the monk had two completely blue eyes. Pale blue, the entire eyeball, both. "Are you The Master?" she asked.

"I am." He nodded. "And you have earned yourself an hour before all your work must be destroyed."

8

Will looked out over the cold, frozen expanse of the school grounds, the sun breaking just above the treeline, yawned and decided: *Today is the day.*

He turned back to the crackling fire and well-blotted pages on his night table and was glad to have finished the play. The two lovers escaped, as he would. Sometimes life was like that. And, besides, these days with the plague and the instability of those in power and the worries people had about food and their lives in general, who needed lovers to die? No, there must be a happy ending. Romeo and Juliet must live happily ever after, just as he and Bethsabe would!

Yes, sometimes good things do happen.

Today is the day.

As he began to pack his clothes into the same knapsack he'd brought them in, Will couldn't help but think how much he'd changed during his time at the school. He'd grown. The decision to leave home had been the right one.

Did he feel guilty about leaving his wife and children? No. It was necessary. Perhaps his wife would not be happy about him finding love with another woman but she would have to understand. Besides, the glory he was bound for in London – hadn't they all said it? He was a genius! – would be sufficient for her. She would have his name and his money. The children would be looked after. He would have done his job.

"Are you leaving, sir?"

"I am," said Will, looking at the boy in the doorway. "You?"

"No."

Romeo was very thin and had a head of thick, dark hair. His eyes were bright from his reading. All he'd done since arriving at the school was study and learn. He'd told Will he wanted nothing more to do with the cruel world which had given him his love and taken her away. Instead he would take refuge in stories. In imaginary worlds. In his own imagination. "I am but a figment of God's imagination," he'd taken to saying.

"Leave the books now, boy. You've studied well." Will forced a pair of boots into the bag. "Besides, the weather is about to worsen again. The farmers in the *Benbow* last night could hardly drink for moaning. Blizzards the likes of which we've never seen are on the way, apparently. In a matter of hours."

"I may stay here," Romeo answered. *I have nowhere else to go.*

"You'll freeze, boy."

"So be it."

Will locked eyes with him. "Don't be too brave for your own good. There's a big world out there, you know. Pack up your things and go out and find your fortune."

"There's nothing out there for me," came the answer. "It's all here." He tapped his heart.

"If it's love that's got you so down, love can put you back on your feet," Will said. He straightened and slapped his hand against his own forehead. He was completely bald on the crown now. What was left of his hair was wispy brown and curled around his ears, half-obscuring the rakish gold ring he still insisted on wearing. "I forgot to tell Mrs Sharpe about the tunnel."

"I can do it, sir."

Will thought about this and shook his head. "No, if you really intend on staying here, lad, read the play. It's finished and I'd appreciate your comments. It's your story, after all, in circumstance if not setting."

Romeo walked across to the table. Turning the pile of crisp papers over he began to read from the final Exeunt backwards. "But – they live?" he exclaimed, turning to see his Master had left the room. Snow was beginning to fall again, some of it drifting silently in through the open doorway. "But they cannot live," Romeo said to himself, going back to the script, shaking his head.

Will reached the Master's house and banged on the door. "Mrs Sharpe! Mrs Sharpe!"

"She's away drowning kittens," came a voice, and Will turned to see Ezekiel the Reeve glaring out at him from under a snow-speckled hood.

"I see, sir."

"You're young Will, aren't you?"

"I am, sir."

"Well, I was coming to see you, too. You'll best be making your way off to town soon. The road'll be impassable in an hour."

Will looked up at the sky. A few flakes but it didn't look so bad. "The London Road, sir?"

"That's it. Those who wish to stay should make themselves known to me at the inn. I'd thank you to be kind enough to pass on the message." He turned his horse. "Must hurry. Much to do."

"Thank you kindly, good sir. Godspeed."

Will wandered out towards the frozen-over allotments and black pond, the grass whitening before his eyes. Suddenly the air was wild with snow.

As he was about to turn back towards the ruins and his room, he noticed, through the trees, out on the meadow, a dark shape in the snow. Was it Mrs Sharpe again? With Bess perhaps?

He glanced back. The snow was falling but not yet critical. "Damn it." He strode out past the pond, over the furrows, by the stumpy, dying plants and noticed, coming closer, that what was in the meadow was a human figure. A nude human figure. Short, dark hair and bare flanks. "Romeo!" Will shouted. "Romeo, no!"

He should have known the boy was unstable, of unsound mind. What was he doing thinking he could look after someone like that? He had abandoned his own children and now he thought he could take care of a troubled youth?

Will stopped and a series of terrible thoughts crossed his mind. Leave him there, exposed. Let him perish. Leave him to God. It's for the best. The boy was damaged. Unfixable. Ashes to ashes, dust to dust.

Will turned to go back – wild billows of snow blocking out his views of the remains of the Abbey – but immediately knew he couldn't do it. That boy was like him. They were brothers, as all of humanity were brothers and sisters. Yes, the boy was like a son, but also like a brother. Of the same mind. In need of the same help. Love.

Will turned and began to run through the blizzard. He wanted to cry out but the wind was too strong in his face: my word, where had this evil storm come from? The top of the world? Angry at having been alone for so long?

As he finally reached Romeo, guided by the flash of black hair he saw through the white, broken blankets, he was shocked to see the figure in the snow was a girl. A young girl. Naked, cold, almost purple. She had a glassy, dazed expression on her face. "H-he-hello," she tried, though trembling lips.

Will took off his coat and wrapped it around her shoulders. As she tried to pull it around herself he noticed she was carrying something in her hand. An acorn, was it? It seemed very green, almost lurid, against her grey, dead-looking palm and the snow.

"Who are you? What's your name, lass?"

Gillian looked at him and a light shone behind her cold face as the answer came to her. "Juliet."

"Juliet?" Will looked about, was this some kind of joke? He thought of his play. Who had put the maid up to this? With the wind beginning to howl, he made the girl stand up and shouted into her face, "Whom do you seek here?"

"Romeo."

"Romeo," Will repeated. "Of course, of course. Ha! Why would it be anything else?"

Gillian smiled and seemed blissfully ignorant of the weather.

"Oh! Is he here?"

Will looked down at her bare legs and purple feet. "You must come with me. You're going to freeze to death but you're not going to freeze to death here and now."

Without ceremony he lifted the girl in his arms and carried her, stamping through the snow until he saw a treeline and realised he'd got his bearings wrong. He was at the outer limits of the school, at The Dips, where they'd buried the Master. But – oh! – yes! There was a small storage area here, a tiny shelter. That would do.

He ploughed on, the girl murmuring against his neck. Finally the faint outline of his goal came into view. This was where they kept the plough and reins dry, out of the rain. It was little more than three pieces of vertical wood and a metal sheet for a roof but it was something. It would do until he could get back to the Abbey and his room and bring blankets.

There was already a layer of snow, like icing on a cake, on the iron roof and Will sought out sacks, boards and anything else that might keep the girl warm. "You must stay here. Try to keep warm. I will go and bring your Romeo to you."

"He is here?" Gillian asked. She was so numb she was in no pain. "Really?"

"I will get him. Stay here. Try to stay warm. Save your energy. Stay warm, I beseech you. I beg you, remain here. I will bring your love. Stay!"

Will began to back away. He turned and walked as quickly as he could uphill through the thick drifts, looking back only once to see the girl standing under the shelter as though made of porcelain.

She'll be frozen solid by the time I get back.

There followed a few minutes of wandering blind before Will saw a light up ahead, moving, which he took to be the sun. But it wasn't. Night was falling and it was a lantern. He lifted his coat over his head, ducked down and drove himself on.

As he got closer to the light, drawn like a moth, Will noticed there were figures beneath the glowing orb, well-wrapped-up figures leaning their way through the angry snowstorm just like him. One was Mrs Sharpe, he saw. The other, Will could tell by the body shape, was Ayland, and the third – oh, the third was Bethsabe. Will could smell her: smell the sweet perfume which turned his stomach inside out, even in that cold, in that storm.

Buoyed by this vision, close now, Will was about to shout out to them when he noticed something which turned his blood as cold as the weather. The tall figure of the aristocratic youth had his arm around the waist of his Bethsabe and, as Will watched, his precious love turned her face to the young man's and they kissed and laughed with such an expression of pure joy that Will fell to the snow on his knees in pain. No vision in the world could have hurt him more.

He could taste snow in his mouth, feel his ears burning with the cold.

That didn't happen. My mind is playing tricks on me.

Will scrambled to his feet and went after them, after that high, jiggling ball of fiery light flickering through the fast falling snow. He caught up with them again. Ayland's hand – *fiend!* – was indeed on his beloved's waist. He heard laughter from fat old Mrs Sharpe, cackling like a witch.

"He'll keep churning them out all right," she was crowing. "I've seen his type before."

"As long as we don't let him freeze," Ayland said.

"I think I shall rather like London," Bethsabe came in, pulling out her dress and dancing a joyful jig in the snow.

Will let himself fall back and stopped walking. Once again he collapsed. Knees, hands, face.

This time he didn't get up.

It was comfortable lying there.

Everything slowly faded away.

9

"Fishing," Kizzie laughed, shaking her head.

She and Zak were walking arm in arm down the lane which ran behind the pavilion. They could have turned and walked up to the village and St Catherine's Church or they could walk down to the bypass, which they did.

"What's wrong with catching something for our supper?" Zak laughed.

"What? Like a tyre?"

"I was thinking more like diphtheria."

The brown, winter boughs interlocked like bony fingers above them. They walked hand in hand, neither of them speaking. *Perhaps he knows what's going to happen*, Kizzie thought. Each time she wanted to say something, she couldn't. They walked on in silence, alongside the empty meadows, alongside the empty village rugby pitch, with its leaning white posts and rickety changing room shed. At the bypass they walked half a mile up the busy road and then under it, via a stinking underpass.

"People come from miles around to use this as a toilet," Kizzie said.

"Roomy," agreed Zak.

On the other side of the tunnel was farmland and a railway bridge. They crossed a stile and walked hand in hand over squidgy grassland to a bend in the river, half-mindful of the dumb, cud-chewing cows watching them from a slimy spot on the far side. Hills rose up around and about them like the stands of a green coliseum.

They stood on the bank of the river and looked down at it. It was shallow and brown, the colour of treacle but transparent. There were no fish in sight but insects skittered on the surface. There were eddies and reeds and as they looked into the drifting liquid they both remembered legends about a second, deeper river under this one, parallel to it, further underground. It went on for miles, people said, like a snake or tapeworm, creeping in a slow brown line just under the chalk hills, around stepping stones, through vineyards and meadows and under houses, onwards and outwards to the sea.

"Can I show you something?" Zak asked, sitting down once he'd checked the grass was dry.

"Of course."

"Look." He rolled up the leg of his school trousers and both stared at nothing. There was nothing there. No leg. It was as if his limb stopped with his trousers. This might not have seemed so strange if his shoe had not been sitting flat on the grass complete with pulled-up grey sock.

"Where's your leg?" asked Kizzie and covered her mouth as though about to laugh.

"It was like this when I woke up this morning. I noticed it in the shower. No one said anything on the run. I don't know if they didn't see it or what, but no one said anything. But you can see it, right? I couldn't even ask Sol."

Kizzie held out her hand. "May I?"

"Be my guest."

She waved her hand through the space where Zak's leg should have been. "Oh, wow."

Zak dropped his trouser leg. "Please tell me if you know what's happening to me, Kiz. I don't know why, but I think you do. I hope you don't, but I think you do."

Tears popped up in the sockets of Kizzie's blue eyes. "I'm so sorry, Zak. I love you so much."

"Tell me what's happening to me. Did you put on a spell on me? Sol says Priya told him you're into black magic and stuff."

"White magic. And, no. I didn't."

"Then what is it?"

Kizzie swallowed hard. They seemed to be the only people in the world. "I made you up," she said.

Zak continued to stare into her eyes as he thought about this. The strangest reaction of all – a smile – began to form on his face. "That's why I can't remember anything properly." He nodded to himself.

"I'm so sorry."

Zak turned back to her. "I didn't know what was wrong with me."

"I did a bad thing. I know. I've been told so many times now. I know I did wrong. I shouldn't have made you do this. Come here."

"But if you hadn't done it, I wouldn't have met you," Zak replied. He looked genuinely happy, which made Kizzie burst into tears like a baby robbed of a toy. "What? What are you so upset about?" He took her hand and she fell against his shoulder and chest, bawling.

"You're going to go away!"

Zak might have said "no", but then he remembered his leg and could only nod. "I can't remember where I came from but it can't have been so bad, can it?" He felt at peace for the first time in a long while, looked up at the sky sparkling through the treetops and sought out a quick, brown bird hiding somewhere, chirruping. He breathed in the smell of the river, of Kizzie's hair and the gentle, cold, autumn breeze which blew over them. "This is so special. Now I know."

"I don't want you to go."

Zak lifted her head off his chest and made her look at him. "But you made me up, Kizzie. You just said it. I can't go anywhere, can I? I'll always be with you."

"But I want you here! Here! So I can hold your..." But as she was about to say "hand" she saw he was going.

"This is it, then," he said.

Kizzie crouched down, hugged her own kneecaps and broke down. "Oh, no!"

When she looked up, wiping her face, it was colder and there was a pile of clothes beside her: a hat and a pair of cowboy boots.

"Zak?"

Standing, she saw splashes, splashes that could only have been made by someone stepping through the stream, whitening the water's surface.

"Zak, is that you?"

From the opposite bank came the sound of someone climbing out of the water. The grass was flattened, scratches appeared in the mud bank and then the longer reeds were flattened. Higher up the bank, saplings moved and bent as though an invisible body were pushing through them.

"Goodbye, my love," Kizzie said quietly, picking up his clothes.

10

"Master Shakespeare!"

Romeo pulled at the dark collar he'd recognised and turned the body over.

Will's face was very pink, the tip of his nose black with frostbite and his nostrils and eyelashes choked with snow but he was breathing. Romeo hauled him up onto his own shoulders and began to crunch back towards the ruins. It was dark but the night was still and calm. The full moon hung directly ahead, staring down like a lidless eye, and stars popped out in the darkness as the sun fell behind the earth.

Will's room was warm and busy with bodies. Mrs Sharpe jumped to her feet as Romeo returned. "He's found him!" she cried. "The lad's found him! Oh, blessed be God, the boy has found him!" Bethsabe and Ayland also brightened.

"Dear Master Shakespeare!" Ayland cried.

"You live!"

Will was insensible. His fingers were like ice but Romeo had reached him just in time. Mrs Sharpe knew well enough not to put him too close to the fire but to let him thaw and warm up slowly, as naturally as possible. Once their original elation had died away, Romeo watched as the three of them discussed what best to do, in low voices.

"Perhaps I should go on ahead?" Ayland said. "There looks to be no more snow tonight. I shall go up to London, or as far as I can, and smooth things over for when you decide to follow." He touched Bethsabe's hand.

"I don't want to leave you," the dark lady answered in a whisper. Will, his face turned to the wall, might not have heard it, but Romeo, standing just inside the doorway, did. Seeing a look of disgust creeping onto his face, Bethsabe barked, "You'd best not be caring about any business which isn't yours, boy."

Mrs Sharpe joined in. "Get your things and go, you little bugger," she told Romeo in a firm, cold voice. "Your studies here are complete. There's no more food to feed you and you're not wanted. Go on – *git!*"

"Wait."

All of them turned at the weak voice which had emanated from the bed. Will rolled onto his side and tried to smile at Bethsabe. Romeo, seeing this, wanted to shout at him – *They don't care about you! It's all a trap! They only want your plays!* – but Bethsabe was already over by the red-faced Will, kneeling, resting her head on his cold hands and crying crocodile tears of joy that Will had survived. "I thought the Lord had taken back a genius!" she cried.

"Not yet," croaked Will.

"The snow's not the best place to sleep, my friend," Ayland chimed in.

Will groaned. "At least it caught me when I fell."

"I'll bring soup!" Mrs Sharpe declared, pushing rudely past Romeo in the doorway.

"You should go to London tonight," Will told Bethsabe as she stared at him as though he were one of the wonders of the world.

"Leave, my love? Without you?"

"I'm not fit to travel."

"The snow will return."

"We will all go," Ayland declared proudly. "Or none at all. And let that be the last word on it."

"Noble sentiments," Will managed. "But, no. There's no sense in it. Take the play. It is finished."

"Sir, no!" Romeo could not stand back and watch this happen.

"Quiet!" Will shouted, with more menace than any of them had thought possible.

"We cannot take the play but not you, sir," Ayland said, but his eyes were on the table. He quickly calculated the distance between himself, Romeo and the script. "Is it really finished?"

He lunged for it and got it before the boy.

"Thief!" growled Romeo. "Sir..." he began, turning to his teacher. "Mr Shakespeare, sir, these two have..."

"Silence!" Will cried, lifting his hand. The exertion made him cough. "Pray you stay silent lest I reprimand you, boy, and then you may stay silent for ever! Feed the fire. Make yourself useful."

Romeo backed down. He went towards the flames and knelt before them, puzzled but compliant.

"Go to London as I say," Will told Bethsabe. "It is my wish. If you love me, you will do it." He turned to the tall youth. "Ayland? Will you look after my love?"

"As a sister, sir."

"Truly, a man did never have a better friend."

Ayland bowed. Bethsabe managed more tears and protestations but she finally allowed Ayland to drag her away from Will's bed and wailed until she was safely in the carriage, trotting out the through the slush and out of the school grounds.

"Please, sir?" Romeo asked, coming up to the bed. "May I talk? I beg you listen. I know what they are doing. Those people are not what they seem."

"I know well," Will replied, with firmness. "They have betrayed me but I would be a hypocrite if I thought, too, that I had never betrayed anyone. I have betrayed my wife. My children. My marriage vows. My God."

"Sir." Romeo nodded.

"Your Juliet is here," Will said, falling back onto the pillow.

"Beg pardon, sir?"

"Your girl. Your Juliet. She is here. With an acorn in her hand so you know it is her – *she is here!*"

Romeo stared at Will in shock. "Where is she?"

"Where we took you to build not two days past."

"There?" asked Romeo, almost falling over in his hurry to get out of the room. "Are you sure, sir?"

"There," nodded Will, his eyes closing.

Romeo backed out into the frozen night and ran to his room. It was a cold cell at the end of a nearby tunnel thronged with bats. Romeo knelt on the cold, dirty sheets and worked out a brick above the headboard with the knife he always carried on his belt. From the vacated space he withdrew a roll of cloth and in the centre of the cloth he let the acorn, which Gillian had given him at their wedding, roll into the palm of his hand.

And then he set out across the ice, running as fast as he could.

11

Kizzie walked back into the school grounds feeling older. *So I'm back where I started,* she thought, remembering the first day she and Athy had been brought to St Francis's by their parents, almost seven years earlier. Not much had changed. They had all grown older but the school had remained the same. The school was the sun the student and teacher bodies swirled around.

Kizzie felt she had learned her lesson. She knew what she wanted now – love – and she knew that she had the ability to affect the lives of many other people and that she had to be careful with that responsibility. But for now the main thing she wanted was peace and quiet. Calmness. A simple life. Get up, go to class, work hard, pass her exams, do some sport and go to bed. She thought about lying on her bed in the dorm reading a good book and it sounded like heaven. It really was the simple things in life that gave you the most pleasure, she thought.

A voice that seemed to come from the trees overhead whispered, *Patience.*

As Kizzie walked on, thinking of this, wondering what her life had in store for her, she noticed Angela standing outside the Main Building hugging someone. It was another girl, a woman, Kizzie noticed, who looked just like Angela. The woman waved and got into a car and drove away as Kizzie walked up to her friend. Angela was in sports clothes, a navy hoodie and white trainers.

"I didn't know you had a sister," Kizzie said.

"Ha! That's my mum!"

"No way. She looked about twenty."

"Thirty-three. She had me when she was very young." Angela leaned against the wall and stretched her thigh. "You up for a walk? I don't want to go up yet."

"Course," said Kizzie. It was a dry, quiet day. The school seemed oddly deserted, although most pupils would be on the other side of the Main Building, in the dining hall, the library or indoors. The two girls followed the route of the driveway, down past the Day Girl's House to the workmen's sheds and the perimeter wall.

"It's been crazy this term, hasn't it?" Angela said.

"Nuts."

"Are you all right?" Angela looked up at her friend.

"I think so." Kizzie grinned. "You?"

"My mum just told me she's pregnant," Angela said. "She only got married about two years ago. He's a businessman. He's nice. But she's *pregnant*."

"That's good though, isn't it?"

"It's weird!"

"You're going to have a brother or sister!"

"Sister." Angela laughed and looked up at the sky. "She just found out. Came straight here to tell me, she said."

"But that's great, Ange! Isn't it?"

"Yes, yes." Angela bit her fingernails. "I've just been on my own so long, you know. I've just got used to it, that's all. Doesn't seem real. Seems like I'm a bit old, you know."

"My dad always says, 'there are no rules'," Kizzie replied. "My mum doesn't agree. She says if there were no rules there'd be anarchy, but my dad says that at the bottom of everything, there are no rules. You can't be too old to have a sister because there's no such thing as too old, do you know what I mean?"

They were walking along the perimeter wall. "I wonder if she'll come here?" Angela wondered aloud. They were walking into The Dips now, towards the two interlocking sycamore trees. "Do you reckon the school will be here then?"

"Ha! This place? This place will be here in a hundred years. A thousand!"

"Probably," agreed Angela. As they came out from behind

the shelter of the buildings she shivered in the wind. "I'm going to go back and have a shower. What have we got later?"

"English. Finishing the play."

Angela pulled a face. "Oh, great. Are you coming?"

Kizzie was standing under the sycamores and as she looked up and around herself, she spoke her thoughts aloud: "No, I'm gonna stay here a minute."

"Sure?"

"Sure."

Kizzie watched Angela walk towards the sixth form block with her hands in her pockets, walked across to the first sycamore tree and touched the gnarly bark.

"I love you wherever you are," she said in a quiet voice. She turned her face to the grey-blue sky and closed her eyes, letting the gentle, cold wind blow over her skin. For a moment, when she opened her eyes, everything was whiter than usual and it seemed like the leaves were talking to her. She stepped across to the other trunk and repeated her words. "I love you all. Wherever you are."

And then, when she was ready, she walked back to school.

Angela showered and was changing when the bell rung. As usual she had thought a lot in the shower. For some reason ideas came to her in the shower. Now she dried herself as quickly as she could, irritated, as usual, that she had to dry herself. *How come they can invent bombs and washing machines and spaceships but they can't invent something that can dry you after a shower?*

In the dorm she pulled on her green tights and remembered the plan she'd come up with. Yes, it still seemed possible. Still made sense.

Angela had been thinking about what Leana had said, about how there might be a writer in the family, about how it didn't have to be her – and she'd decided that all the strange things that had been happening were connected to her new sister. She wanted to write something for her sister but she also wanted to test Leana's theory. If what Leana said, and what they all believed at the school, this would all make sense. If not, it wouldn't. After the weirdness she'd been through these last few days she was leaning towards thinking there was some truth in it all.

With her wet hair dripping onto the paper, Angela scrawled out a note to her sister who hadn't even been born yet. She kept it simple:

If strange things are happening to you and you feel like you've got no one to talk to and you don't understand what's happening, remember you can always talk to me. I was here once, like you, and strange things happened to me. You're not crazy. Wherever I am, come and talk to me and I'll tell you what's happening. Don't feel alone. Don't feel like you're going mad. I am your sister and I love you. Find me.

She finished. "I'm nuts."

Angela combed her hair fast, shaking her head at the typically rotten state of her skin, folded the note and walked out into the corridor. It was empty. She could hear the last of the girls banging down the main stairs, going to class and she looked about. Where to hide the note?

The Common Room was the most obvious place. She looked at the old furniture. Yes, it had been there years but there was no way it was going to be there in twenty years' time – no way. The floorboards creaked but putting something under them was too risky. There were pipes and leaks and, besides, she'd have to dig them up or pull them up and she didn't have time.

From the window she looked out over the back lawn, the school pond, swimming pool and Assembly Hall. Down below, groups of students walked the pathways in groups, rucksacks slung from their shoulders, boys teasing the girls, girls flicking their hair.

What is never going to change about this place? she thought. Looking around the room she saw some dusty old volumes on one of the shelves and walked across to them. Books?

She read along the spines. They were old editions with some new books squeezed in, even some homework sheets and old exams. There were CDs and DVDs and a broken mobile phone, the screen smashed like a cobweb, and there was *The Collected Works of William Shakespeare*. Angela laughed. *Of course!*

She drew down the book and flicked open the cover.

This book belongs to Enid Waters, it said.

"Who?"

Angela felt time pressing down on her and closed her eyes. She flicked through the pages, smelling the musty, dusty age of the book, and slipped her note into a random page. Although she didn't want to, she had to peep at the name of the play she'd chosen. It was *Julius Caesar*. "Oh, no," she said, flipping on to *Anthony and Cleopatra* and nodding. "Cleopatra, better." She slid the note in between the pages.

"Right, then. Let's see."

Back went the book, into its place. Angela wiped the dust off her hands, picked up her bag, slung it over her shoulder and walked across the creaking floorboards to the door. She glanced back once, just to check she hadn't moved anything she shouldn't have, and then left.

From the empty Common Room you could hear her footfalls on the stairs as she raced downwards to class.

And then there was nothing, only an old clock ticking.

The clock, as it always had and always would, was showing the wrong time.

12

Alain followed his heart.

All was ice and night had fallen. He was more afraid than he thought he'd be at being here, at having given up his life to find Gillian again, but now that he was here, what could he do? He had to find her. Had to tell her how he felt. He had to convince her to love him again.

The ground was knee-deep in snow although the blizzard had stopped. The sky was somewhere above, watching; the full moon glaring down and lighting everything silverfish grey.

The trees cast grim shadows and, in the distance, Alain made out the leaning, tired fence which marked the boundary of the school. He'd studied his history; he knew the way the school had grown, where the old road ran. He'd read the legends of the site, of the ancient churches and Roman forts, of all that had happened here, in this weird little corner of the grounds which had somehow resisted ever being built on.

And then he saw the grave. The burial mound.

He felt as sad as he'd ever felt in his life; great sadness like a blow. He'd made Kizzie write that she must take him to Gillian and here he was. But he was too late. She was dead. Worse, because the soil on the mound had less snow on it than on the surrounding land – it was warm! Fresh! – she was recently dead! Recently gone! He'd been too slow. His indecision had killed her!

Alain collapsed, falling to his knees and crying out in frustration. He buried the torch he'd been carrying into the highest point of the mound, sheer brute strength overcoming nature's best attempt to freeze the earth.

"Oh, my love! Gillian! I came back for you!" With red eyes Alain stared up at the sky and shouted at God and fate for bringing him here late, for not allowing him to be with his love at all. "Oh, but you taught me love," he said, addressing the grave, suddenly realising that she had – *she really had.*

He dug out a G in the snow, deep and bold. "You taught me what it is to love without giving me even a kiss. Without touching me. And now I know what love is. It's not gentle and sweet but rough and painful. Now I know. And I know because of you."

Alain lay with his head on the cold, hard soil and noticed an approaching torchlight. Someone was coming.

He stood up, acting on instinct, withdrawing into the flickering shadows, crouching next to the trunk of a tree, which might have been a witch. It was alive and sharp and watched with him as Romeo arrived, sinking into the snow on each step, panting hard.

What's this? Romeo thought, noticing the dying embers of Alain's torch being gradually snuffed out by the frost. And he saw what could only be a burial mound: there were dead flowers pressed into it, rimed with hoary frost, quite beautiful. Someone had left a cup nearby. In the snowy rise he saw the letter G which Alain had traced out and dropped to his knees as though before an altar.

"No!"

Without thinking of what he was doing, Romeo began to claw at the dirt, ignoring the pain, pulling great handfuls of frozen ground away and throwing them over his shoulder, behind him, anywhere, thinking: *She may still be alive in there! I will claw her back from death! Death cannot defeat this love I feel!*

"No!" Alain dived onto the other boy's shoulders and Romeo, growling wildly, rolled them both over backwards and sprang to his feet.

"Get back!" Romeo pulled out a short, sharp dagger. "Honestly, man. Get back. Stay away from me. I'll cut you open."

"She's dead, you idiot! Dead!"

"Get back!" Spittle and desperation shot out into the circle of darkness between the two men as they turned in a strange dance. Alain, too, had armed himself. He had a small pickaxe he'd found on the floor by the tree.

"No good will come of digging up a grave, believe me," Alain said, half-crouching.

"I'm begging you to leave me alone. I can't answer for what I will do to you if you do not leave me alone." Romeo was pleading. "Just walk away and all will be well."

"You will leave her in peace now." Alain swallowed hard. "We both must. She's gone. What's done is done. Leave her in peace. Leave her to God."

"Get away from me!" screamed Romeo, lunging at Alain with the knife. He held it high above his head and brought it down so close to Alain's ear that the Frenchman heard wind.

"Are you mad? How much death do you want tonight?"

"For the last time," the other boy answered, still turning, "take your leave, man, and let me stay here in peace."

"If you touch that grave I'll make sure you're punished."

"You have no authority here!" Romeo jerked the knife. "You've got no authority anywhere, you fool."

"You will pay for your actions, boy! I promise you that!"

"I don't care!" Romeo lunged in again, catching Alain in the thigh. Alain tried to bring the pickaxe down but Romeo saw it – he was so alive, his senses on fire, that the axe seemed to come at him in slow motion.

A split second after he'd ducked, the sharp blade he thrust went in under Alain's trailing, flailing arm and buried its blade snug between the boy's exposed ribs. The sharp metal pierced Verne's heart and – eyes wide open in shock – the leader of the Magistrate fell and was dead before he hit the cold earth.

Romeo took his knife, wiped it clean and sheathed it. The adrenalin was already beginning to wear off, his fingers and knees trembling, and he took himself back to the grave and stood before the mound thinking dark thoughts. He had a knife.

His life was no longer worth living.

From the lightening gloaming beyond he saw what might have been eyes lit by the dying torchlight. Watching eyes. The glint of a fox's eye, or a wolf's. But no.

"Gillian?"

Romeo walked around the mound and shook his head in disbelief. There was a body on the snowy ground under a small shelter, the head slightly inclined. Her body. It was her! Romeo raced across. Gillian was pale, very grey, her eyes wide open. Romeo held her close but she was rigid and cold. "My love!"

He tried to hold her but her clothes seemed attached to the ground, stuck to it. Throughout all this she stared as though hypnotised.

"My love, my love."

Romeo took her hand, pulled open the fingers and cried out in pain and recognition when he saw the small acorn, still warm, in her grey palm.

"My wife, my darling wife," he said, whispering, kissing her frozen cheek. "My soul. My reason. My everything!"

Romeo did his best to gather her clothes about her but there was no way to do it without tearing them so he began to remove his own, placing them over her body, feeling the cold but not caring. Eventually he was as naked as he'd been on the first day he'd come into this odd world, trembling at the terrible cold, which began to burn him inside and out, but not caring.

"Look, my love," he told her, with his purple lips next to hers. In his hand he had his own acorn: their wedding gift. "Like our love, we will always be together now."

And he lay there, with her, on top of her, next to her, until he froze to death.

It was sometime in the night, a lonely private time when the stars oscillate and the planets hum, when Gillian opened her eyes. The first thing she saw was her husband: his eyes, just like the first time. But now they would never close again. They were frozen open, locked by death.

She noticed his clothes on her. Realised what must have happened.

Gillian had come back from somewhere to see him, that she knew. But she was too late. He had gone, gone ahead of her, and now she must follow. Now she would join her husband in death's kingdom. The saddest loneliest place in the world would be like heaven if they were both there. Yes, it would! They must be together in death.

This place, this world, was not where she should be. It never had been.

It was not the world itself – the world was not interested in love or people, it was indifferent. The world was a wild thing, like the sea, like life, like moods, like love. No, it was to be human in the world. That was the difficult thing. Never far from love, perhaps, but also always close to illness, fear and death. There was no escape from this world if you were human, she thought. Love eases the way to death. All is death.

They had tamed love together. Tamed it and been forever bonded by it. Gillian believed that. Both of them had believed their vows. Theirs was a bond that had crossed different zones of consciousness and now it would cross the ultimate barrier. Gillian was convinced of it.

She must go and be with him. Go and be with her husband. Go to where their love would save them.

She took the small dagger from her husband's belt and raised it methodically, to a height she instinctively knew would be enough, before bringing it down into her body, taking herself back to him.

Back to *them*.

Sunday

Dawn arrived like good news.

Darkness and shadows became colour and form.

The night and storm withdrew, sucked back to the high hills and into the sky. The snow glowed with warm, red light and the sound of the day breaking woke a sparrow which hadn't sung for months.

Will Shakespeare, lying face down beside the small, frozen pond, lifted his frost-encrusted face and could hardly believe such night had ever ended. He could hardly believe he'd survived.

Groaning, he stared at the frozen pond before him and, with a dirty fingernail, scratched out his signature on its frosty surface. It was an instinctive action, proving to himself he was alive; that he'd made it through the night.

I must leave here, he thought. *The boy is gone.*

He had searched all night, until exhaustion had grounded him. The blizzard had stopped him making it right down to The Dips and he'd fallen in his tracks not really knowing where he was. The wind had been fierce and blinding. Nothing and nobody could have survived in those conditions.

Will muttered a prayer. He could sense he was alone. He knew Romeo and Juliet were gone.

There is nothing left for me here. I have the play. I must carry on.

Will thought of his wife and children. He loved them. He would make them proud.

I will use everything that happens to me in life to make my writing better.

He thought of Bethsabe and smiled ruefully.

Yes, I will write about you, too.

Ah, humans were strange animals. Brothers and sisters, children of the earth, always fighting and squabbling and desperate to see the differences among themselves rather than the similarities. So quick to oppose and divide; so slow to understand and forgive. Always fighting – between countries, between religions, within families, among siblings, friends and neighbours. And weren't humans always fighting in their hearts, too?

But they could love and what was life without love? Without feeling? Without moments of enervating, shimmering, wonderful thought and sensation? What was life without emotion? Without tears, joy, suffering and triumph?

The young lovers are dead, Will concluded, adding quickly, *but then everyone dies in the end.*

As the first, warm beams of sunlight reached him and coaxed the heat back into his bones, those words suddenly felt very profound. He thought of his play, of the story of his student Romeo and the girl Juliet, and knew what he must do: what he must change.

Let the others have their romantic twaddle: it was the pain of love that was universal! That is what he would write about. That is what would take London by storm!

Everyone dies in the end!

Will got to his feet and was about to set off when he heard a crack from somewhere nearby. It was the ice in the pond, breaking under pressure from the fingers of the sun.

You will always be here with us, as will I. It is written. I have written it.

You must write on the moon before you leave here, before you can leave here.

A part of you will always be here with us, as will I.

Neither of us shall never truly leave. Myself in spirit, you in words and deeds.

Write on the moon and watch it disappear.

Will watched his name sink away and the reflection of the full moon took its place on the surface of the dark, rippling water.

He looked up at the ruins, lit like a golden temple by the rising sun, and began to walk in the opposite direction, heading for the London road.

As he came through The Dips he saw The Master's grave but paid no attention to the three unremarkable humps in the snow nearby. Hungry, skinny dogs yapped at him as he took off his hat. "It is done, Master." Will walked past the burial mound and out of the school without looking back. "Adieu."

Down in The Dips the snow would melt.

Poor Alain's corpse became breakfast for the dogs as it lay on slightly higher ground and the thin layer of snow covering his grave melted first. Sated, and with plenty of other food available from the other buildings, the strays left the two remaining bodies long enough for the acorns Romeo and Gillian had lain on, clutched tightly to their bellies, to sprout.

Slowly the lovers' corpses rotted and were picked apart and eaten away but the acorns made the earth their home, burying their roots deep in the red soil to grow towards the sun together until, many years later, the two trunks interlocked and the two lovers became one again, somewhere between heaven and earth.

In the end, even death could not part them.

Also by the Author

The Invisible Hand
(Lodestone Books 978-1-78535-498-4)

The Invisible Hand is about a boy, Sam, who has just started life at a boarding school and finds himself able to travel back in time to medieval Scotland. There he meets a girl, Leana, who can travel to the future, and the two of them become wrapped up in events in *Macbeth*, the Shakespeare play, and in the daily life of the school.

The book is the first part of a series called *Shakespeare's Moon*. Each book is set in the same boarding school but focuses on a different Shakespeare play.

James Hartley was born in Heswall, on the Wirral, England, on a rainy Thursday in 1973. He's lived in Singapore, Oman, Scotland, Thailand, Libya, Syria, Ireland, France and Germany during his forty-odd years on the planet and has worked as a journalist, waiter, child-minder and dishwasher. He lives in Madrid, Spain, with his wife and two children and teaches English.

You can contact James at james@jameshartleybooks.com

Recent bestsellers from Lodestone Books are:

AlphaNumeric
Nicolas Forzy
When dyslexic teenager Stu accidentally transports himself into a world populated by living numbers and letters, his arrival triggers a prophecy that pulls two rival communities into war.
Paperback: 978-1-78279-506-3 ebook: 978-1-78279-505-6

Shanti and the Magic Mandala
F.T. Camargo
In this award-winning YA novel, six teenagers from around the world gather for a frantic chase across Peru, in search of a sacred object that can stop The Black Magicians' final plan.
Paperback: 978-1-78279-500-1 ebook: 978-1-78279-499-8

Time Sphere
A timepathway book
M.C. Morison
When a teenage priestess in Ancient Egypt connects with a schoolboy on a visit to the British Museum, they each come under threat as they search for Time's Key.
Paperback: 978-1-78279-330-4 ebook: 978-1-78279-329-8

Bird Without Wings FAEBLES
Cally Pepper
Sixteen-year-old Scarlett has had more than her fair share of problems, but nothing prepares her for the day she discovers she's growing wings...
Paperback: 978-1-78099-902-9 ebook: 978-1-78099-901-2

Briar Blackwood's Grimmest of Fairytales
Timothy Roderick
After discovering she is the fabled Sleeping Beauty, a brooding
goth-girl races against time to undo her deadly fate.
Paperback: 978-1-78279-922-1 ebook: 978-1-78279-923-8

Escape from the Past
The Duke's Wrath
Annette Oppenlander
Trying out an experimental computer game, a fifteen-year-old boy
unwittingly time-travels to medieval Germany where he must not
only survive but figure out a way home.
Paperback: 978-1-84694-973-9 ebook: 978-1-78535-002-3

Holding On and Letting Go
K.A. Coleman
When her little brother died, Emerson's life came crashing down
around her. Now she's back home and her friends want to help,
but can Emerson fight to re-enter the world she abandoned?
Paperback: 978-1-78279-577-3 ebook: 978-1-78279-576-6

Midnight Meanders
Annika Jensen
As William journeys through his own mind, revelations are made,
relationships are broken and restored, and a faith that once seemed
extinct is renewed.
Paperback: 978-1-78279-412-7 ebook: 978-1-78279-411-0

Reggie & Me
The First Book in the Dani Moore Trilogy
Marie Yates
The first book in the Dani Moore Trilogy, *Reggie & Me* explores a
teenager's search for normalcy in the aftermath of rape.
Paperback: 978-1-78279-723-4 ebook: 978-1-78279-722-7

Unconditional
Kelly Lawrence
She's in love with a boy from the wrong side of town...
Paperback: 978-1-78279-394-6 ebook: 978-1-78279-393-9

Readers of ebooks can buy or view any of these bestsellers
by clicking on the live link in the title. Most titles are published in
paperback and as an ebook. Paperbacks are available in traditional
bookshops. Both print and ebook formats are available online.

Find more titles and sign up to our readers' newsletter at
http://www.johnhuntpublishing.com/children-and-young-adult.
Follow us on Facebook at https://www.facebook.com/JHPChildren
and Twitter at https://twitter.com/JHPChildren.